A WONDERFUL PLACE TO DIE

MJ BIGGS

For everyone chasing a dream. Don't lose faith in yourself.

CONTENTS

ONE

The rain was merely a muted sprinkling on the waxy fronts of the tree leaves, like salt dropping onto a paper plate. To me, it was quieter than silence, just as the ringing in your ears when you go to bed after being pummeled by the screams of amplifiers and concert-goers.

I sat with my back supported by a rock and my languid hands hanging between my bent knees, far enough in the woods that none of the early walkers or runners could see me from the trail.

A Sonic Youth song came on in my head, as was usual for a damp morning. "Teen Age Riot." I synced my breathing with the intro to quell the urge to throw up again, inhaling when one measure began and exhaling as the next did.

I felt like a thing, an object—used up, grimy, discarded—a greasy napkin left under the driver's seat. And yet, I had never felt so profoundly human.

It was then I realized, staring up into the ceiling of sycamores as if it were written there, that I'd been completely dismantled, and after overanalyzing, I concluded that the dismantlement began when Desmond came into my life.

Everywhere he went, Desmond Carvey glided. His eyes were impenetrable pools of chocolate framed by thick, dark brows. He had lavish, wavy, deep-brown hair to match. He'd comb it back and slightly to his left side. Freckles swept over his angular nose, adding a soft boyishness to an otherwise keen face with a well-carved jawline and subtly concave cheeks. He was tall and lean. His broad shoulders tapered into arms with protruding veins, which slithered down to his strong hands like little serpents under his skin. I thought he was the most beautiful person my eyes had ever beheld, and they were only for him.

We met at a rock club in Cleveland when we were both 16. Our bands happened to be on the same bill one night.

I grew up in the western-most neighborhood of Cleveland, Ohio called West Park—or, more specifically, the Kamm's Corners district of it, a historically-Irish community where people are closely knit.

My street was made up of humble colonial and bungalow homes and lined with scarlet oaks. The grade school I attended, Holy Rosary, was two blocks north of the street, and my high school, an all-girl school called Saint Ambrose Academy, was five blocks north of it.

The Lipinskis lived next door to us. Bernadette Lipinski was my very best friend. Besides her, Mr. and Mrs. Lipinski had two sons, who were close in age to my younger brothers. We spent as much time at one another's houses as we did our own growing up.

Bernadette was tall and slender and walked with a playful buoyancy as though she was floating on the breath of early summer. Her face was heart shaped and her eyes steel blue with flecks of gray, like a pleasantly partly-cloudy sky in June. She recurrently dyed her naturally-medium-brown hair some other brunette or blonde hue.

The two of us discovered Riot Grrrl at the beginning of seventh grade, and that was when I decided I needed to start an all-girl rock band. But first, I had to learn how to play guitar, so I requested an electric guitar for Christmas that year. I convinced Bernadette to learn bass, and she asked for one for her birthday a few months later. We practiced playing together nearly every day with the goal of having band-worthy chops by the time we got to high school.

I also sang lead in the band, which was ironic, because I was terrified of singing in front of people as a kid. I tried out for Holy Rosary's play in junior high and was totally surprised and horrified when I found out during the audition that I'd have to sing. I hadn't known it was a musical. When the casting director struck the first chord to "Happy Birthday" on the piano, it was like my throat was suddenly gobbed up with chunky peanut butter. I could barely make a peep come out. *"Happy Birthday!"* It's not like you were asked to sing "Bohemian Rhapsody," Dani, I said to myself as I secretly sulked in my mom's car on the way home. I got a minor speaking-only part as a result, and I didn't even bother going out for the play the following year. Lo and behold, I'd be belting before hundreds of people on the regular in the near future.

I guess the integrity of my song writing was a bigger concern to me than my stage fright. Creating was my first great love, and I think it was always greater than performing, even when I had the perspective that creating is pointless if the product isn't shown to anyone. I was willing to try working through my fear to ensure that my songs came out the way I imagined them. I didn't want to let somebody else take the reins on them and possibly turn them in different directions. Having bandmates who were my friends and believed in my abilities made that fear much easier to overcome. Once we got past that first bar in the first song of the set, I felt like a queen—cool and in complete control.

For a little while, Bernadette dated the drummer in Desmond's band, Tommy, and the four of us were together all the time. We mostly met Desmond and Tommy where they lived in Lakewood to be farther away from the watchful and protective eyes of our parents and the many people who knew them in our neighborhood. Because Lakewood was so close to our end of West Park, we'd either walk or take the bus.

There was a period in my life when I had to stay away from Lakewood. Its air had a suffocating bitter-sweetness. Simply too much within the city reminded me of being with Desmond—like Angie's, a coffee shop that thought it was a House of Blues, with experimental and psychedelic rock bands blasting its assortment of oversized mugs off the shelves every Thursday through Saturday night. Why the staff never booked artists who played at decibels they could reasonably accommodate— you know, the customary acoustic-guitar-strumming singer-songwriters—I couldn't understand, but the lack of sense in this matter was what made the magic of Angie's atmosphere. Pretty much the entire floor became a stage when a band set up, and the audience members would cram in anywhere they could fit.

Desmond and I always cuddled up to one another on the couch that sat in the front window. We'd get lost in deep, longing looks and an ecstasy of bent notes and flanging, which ricocheted between the narrow walls of the coffee shop and rattled the whole place. I'd see us through the front window when I drove by, and in the punk rock record store three blocks west. We stopped there regularly—usually on our way to someplace else—to browse for rare CDs and vinyls, buy buttons, and pick through the other miscellaneous memorabilia. I'd see us, too, in all the parks where we'd pass time in the summer, and in the venue where we met called Dizzy Dog.

I was carrying my amp to a corner near the stage when I first noticed Desmond. He said hi to me as I pushed the amp against the wall. I was surprised he'd approached me.

"What's your name?" he asked, sliding his hands down into the pockets of his tight, ripped black jeans.

"Dani," I said, reaching out to shake with him.

He looked down at my hand and smirked like it was a weird gesture but shook with me anyway, and I felt like a nerd.

"I'm Desmond," he said. "So what's your band called?"

"Ardis Alchemy," I answered.

"Huh. I dig it. It's original. When do you guys go on?"

"We're playing third."

"Oh, well our band's going on right after yours."

"What's *your* band called?"

"The Stars And You. I take it you play guitar?" he said, eyeing my amp.

"Yes. And I sing," I said.

"What a coincidence—me too." He shifted his focus suddenly to a guy walking up on us. "This is Tommy Boy," he said.

Tommy's cargo shorts were hanging off his hips, and his black shirt fit his twiggy torso like a baby tee. It had one of those generic-sounding metal band names on it, like Death By Plague or something. It wasn't a name I knew.

"What's up?" Tommy said exuberantly to neither of us in particular, cocking his elbow up on Desmond's shoulder and leaning into him.

"This is Dani," Desmond said. "Her band is going on before us."

"Oh, cool!" said Tommy, grinning. He studied me for a moment with this look of wonder, his eyes shining and his mouth open, like he was waiting for me to do some trick and amaze him.

"I should probably go see if there's any more equipment to bring in," I said.

"All right. I'll catch you later. I'm really looking forward to watching you," said Desmond.

I said, "Yeah. Later. And thanks. Me too. I mean, I'm looking forward to watching you too. Bye." Then, my stomach fluttering, I hurried back outside to find Bernadette and our drummer, Gabby.

"That's everything, Dan," Gabby said, closing the trunk of her car.

We went back inside and got cups of water at the bar.

Feeling someone staring at me, I looked up. There was Desmond on the other side of the bar. He held his eye contact forwardly. I felt a giggle coming on—a nervous habit—so I broke the gaze, but I still couldn't prevent myself from smiling that beaming kind of smile. I stared into my lap in hopes that Desmond wouldn't see.

The bouncer called out for everyone who wasn't in a band to line up outside the venue so the door man could collect their cover charge before admission. Band members were supposed to line up behind the bouncer so he could mark a "B" on their hands, which let the door man know they didn't need to pay if they re-entered.

All the people were bustling behind our bar stools, making it difficult to scoot out from behind them and get into the long line that had quickly formed, so we decided we'd wait until the line died down some.

"Hey, girls," someone said from over our shoulders, "I told everyone who isn't in a band to go wait outside." I turned around to find the bouncer.

"Oh, but we are in a band," I said.

He stared at me blankly, then replied, "OK, seriously now, you need to leave. Your boyfriends will still be here after you pay."

Vile words began to swirl and swell in my stomach, but before I could throw any of them up on the bouncer, Desmond interjected.

"Their band is called Ardis Alchemy. They're third in the lineup. Go ask the booking agent over there who made it if you don't believe me." Desmond nodded toward the guy with the clipboard and envelopes of ticket money.

"All right. Well don't forget to get your hands marked," said the bouncer in a tone like a warning.

I stewed on the fact that he found it so unbelievable for us girls to be a band the rest of the day, casting him a dirty look each time I passed by. Although, we *were* the only girls playing the show and the only all-female group I was aware of in the local music scene at the time. The bands with all male members were endless. It was boy band after boy band after boy band after boy band, etcetera, etcetera. Of course, they weren't called "boy bands," just "bands," because they were the norm. Girl bands were referred to as such because they were novelties.

I never understood why so few girls were actually in bands when so many came to listen to them. The ones who were in bands were mainly singers. A female with an instrument was most often in the background, shaking a tambourine, mimicking the guitar riff on keyboard for added depth, or playing bass very subtly as if she wasn't really familiar with the instrument, because she wasn't really a bassist at all, but rather, acting as a bassist with as much ability as someone who isn't one can as a favor to a friend or boyfriend in the band to at least prevent the sound from having a hole, because real bassists are nearly impossible to find. And it doesn't hurt that she's easy on the eyes of the audience and looks good in our promo pictures, the boys in the band would think. The older I got, the more often I'd see girls on stage with instruments. A good sign, a good sign, I'd say.

Desmond and I exchanged numbers at the bar and stuck together the rest of the night. He told me to call him before I went to sleep. Our group left right after the boys' set—Gabby for home, and Bernadette and I for my grandparents' house.

TWO

My grandparents also lived in Lakewood, and it was warm outside, so we walked there from the venue. Lakewood is densely populated but small in area, so nothing within it is a very far walk.

Bernadette and I would be helping out in my grandpa's store the next day. Since we started doing it on weekends in junior high before we were old enough to drive, obviously, and because the four of us mutually enjoyed each other's company, Bern and I often spent the night at their house on Friday and Saturday and rode to work with my grandpa.

By eleventh grade, we had both gotten other part-time jobs, but we still helped at the store as much as possible for a little extra cash and to visit. It was an Italian grocery store with a bakery and deli called Carmin's in what had once been an Italian neighborhood on Cleveland's west side. Grandpa Adrian's parents opened it after they came over from Italy.

Carmin was a shortened version of my grandpa's last name, Carmino. Like many European immigrants, his father changed the family's surname to better assimilate.

Grandpa Adrian told me, "My dad didn't want anyone to know we were Italian so they wouldn't discriminate against us. I said to him, 'You look Italian, you sound Italian, and your store might not have an Italian name, but you sell Italian food. Who're ya tryin' to fool?' I do wish we had held onto the language more. Our parents discouraged us from speaking Italian as kids for our protection, so we mostly forgot it. See, immigrants have always had a hard time, though today, there are at least anti-discrimination laws. People are just immigrating here from different places now than they used to is all."

My grandpa went back to the surname "Carmino" in his early adulthood, but he kept the store name the same. He thought it would be strange and confusing to his loyal customers if the name they'd known for so long changed.

Bern and I arrived at my grandparents' house just before the city's curfew of 11 p.m. They were always up late for some reason anyhow. I rang their long, chiming doorbell. We waited for footsteps and the familiar click of the chain bolt as it unlocked.

"Hellooo!" Grandma Vivian bellowed. She had this funny way of dragging out and inverting the end of the word like she was calling into a dark cave to find out if any living humans were inside.

"Hellooo!" Grandpa Adrian echoed from the living room. I could faintly hear the overacted, muffled dialogue of a black and white film. My grandfather loved this cable channel that played nothing but movies made before 1965 or so.

We stepped inside the house and said our hellos.

"I pulled out some leftovers in case you're hungry," said Grandma Vivian.

We were starved.

"There's rigatoni, meatballs, salad, and garlic bread."

The aroma of tomato sauce with hints of onion and garlic lingered in the air of the house as though it had permeated the carpet and window treatments over time. It mingled with the smell of their antique furniture—an aged-wood smell, like that of the brittle, yellowed pages in an old book—creating a scent that I would forever remember when I thought of my grandparents.

Bernadette and I took the middle seats at the dining room table. My grandma set out silverware, porcelain plates heaped with the reheated leftovers, and salad in matching porcelain bowls. As she did, the cross, mano cornuto, and various other charms on the long, gold chain necklace she always wore jangled and clanked together. Her entire ensemble was something she always wore, for that matter. "Grandma Vivian" could have been a clothing brand. *Simple chic for the modern nanna.* Her look was a tunic, often with a glitzy belt or waist sash, leggings or flowy mesh pants, and flats, except when around the house. Then it was slippers. She styled her long, thick, purple-black hair into voluminous and elegant updos with claws or combs, which she did with seemingly little effort.

"Adrian," Grandma Vivian called to the back of my grandpa's armchair, "why don't you come sit with the girls while they eat."

"I'm coming," he answered, standing up to stretch. "I'll take some coffee too please, dear."

My grandpa sat at the head of the table, his usual place, having left the TV on in the living room. He was dressed in his evening attire—a plain-white t-shirt tucked into sweat pants.

His clothing choices were as predictable as my grandma's. During the day, he wore khakis or black dress pants with a sweater or polo tee, depending on the season, and black or tan Sperrys. In my entire life, I never saw him in a pair of jeans. He changed into his sweats and white tee before doing his nightly dumbbell exercises in the living room. They'd be followed by a brisk walk around the neighborhood, which Bernadette and I sometimes accompanied him on. His silver hair was always parted on the side and slicked back.

"OK, coffee's on," my grandma said. "I'm going out for a cigarette while it's brewing, and then I'll join you."

Something I found strange about my grandma was that she had a strict supplement regimen yet was a heavy smoker. It seemed to me that her smoking would cancel out whatever health benefits the supplements provided.

Every morning I ever spent at my grandparents' house, I remember my grandma popping about 10 different vitamins, which she'd wash down with a cup of warm lemon water for optimal absorption. She kept her vitamins in a pill organizer on the kitchen counter. When I was little, I once pulled a chair up to the counter to watch her go about her routine. I stared at the open plastic compartments holding supplements that mostly appeared too large for human consumption.

"Grandma, what are those ones?" I inquired, pointing to the biggest tablets in the container.

"Those are my horse pills," she replied. I thought they were actually for horses and wondered what purpose they could serve her. I never asked though for fear I'd get an answer my little-kid mind couldn't handle. That I'd someday have a need to take livestock pills that might tear up my insides on the way down was already more than I wanted to know.

"So you girls ready to work tomorrow?" Grandpa Adrian asked.

Bernadette and I both gave mhmmms, our mouths too full of food for real words, as the coffee maker gurgled louder and the first drips of coffee pinged in the glass pot.

"Good, good, because I need the two of yas to advertise the lunch specials tomorrow. And I'm sure there'll be some extra bread you can have when you get hungry. Wouldn't want it to go to waste," said Grandpa Adrian with a wink.

My grandfather helped his employees with the bread baking in the morning and would make one loaf specifically for Bernadette and me to snack on throughout the day. He always looked so pleased as we gleefully accepted the plate he'd fixed of freshly-sliced Italian bread encircling butter balls that resembled vanilla ice cream scoops. We liked taking our snack breaks in the stockroom on crates of tomatoes.

Advertising lunch specials consisted of Bernadette and me holding large, white, cardboard signs made from the boxes the pasta was shipped in with yard sticks duct taped to the bottoms. We'd write the specials in red and green Sharpies.

Sometimes, we'd walk up and down the street with our signs, giving big grins and waves to cars and pedestrians. Other times, we'd camp on the corner outside the store, which was at a four-way intersection, and drown out the world with our own conversations, using the signs as privacy screens. There were a few instances when we propped our signs against an outside wall of the store and sat beside them playing acoustic guitars. My grandpa had said it would be an opportune business arrangement for all of us; he'd get more attention for Carmin's, and we'd get more attention for our music.

"Will lasagna be on the lunch menu tomorrow?" I asked him. It was my favorite thing to eat from Carmin's besides the fresh Italian bread, and the spumoni, which Grandpa Adrian made himself in a machine next to the deli counter.

"Lasagna? Yes," he replied. "And I was going to have anchovy and mushroom pizza made just for Bernadette."

Bernadette twisted her face in disgust.

"No, no, no," said Grandpa Adrian, laughing and shaking his head. "We'll have the usual plain and pepperoni, and I'm thinking one with fresh basil, tomatas, and mozzarella." He replaced the "O" at the end of certain words with an "A" when he spoke. It was tomata and potata instead of tomato and potato. I noticed a lot of older people I met had this habit.

When Bern and I weren't advertising lunch specials, we stocked shelves and cleaned. Grandpa Adrian played jazz—mainly swing and crooners—over the speakers he'd installed on the store ceiling and on the drive to work in his black Cadillac with the black leather interior. I developed a great fondness of jazz because of it. The Glenn Miller Orchestra, Benny Goodman, Billie Holiday, Ella Fitzgerald, Andrews Sisters, Frank Sinatra, Dean Martin, and Sammy Davis Jr. gave me a sense of romanticism in the most ordinary things—watching the lines on the street pass from the backseat window of the car, dusting the checkout counter.

Grandma Vivian returned from outside amid a conversation we were having about current events. She placed her pack of cigarettes and lighter on the bar inside their gold-stained, maple liquor cabinet before going into the kitchen. That cabinet was like a pillar of their house; it had always been there. At every family gathering, Grandpa Adrian would make rows of shot glasses on the cabinet bar and fill them with Crown Royal, his liquor of choice. He'd gather all of us around and hand the shot glasses out—even to the kids. Then, he'd make a toast, and we'd raise our glasses and say, "Salute!" After throwing back the whiskey, all the adults would cheer as though one of the kids had just blown out the candles on their birthday cake.

Grandma Vivian came back into the dining room with two coffee mugs. She set one in front of my grandpa and the other before herself at the opposite end of the table.

"So when's your next concert?" she asked.

"In a couple weeks," I answered.

"Well we'd *love* to come see you girls play again. We were so blown away when we saw you. You're just these quiet little girls, and then you get up on stage, and it's just … bang!" she said, throwing her hands in front of her face with a ta-da motion. "Like little pistols, the both of you."

Bern shot me a sideways glance. I knew she wanted to laugh at my grandma's comment but wouldn't until the two of us were alone.

"Where will the concert be?" asked Grandpa Adrian.

"At Flanders'. We're opening for a national act," I said.

"A national act, huh?" said Grandma Vivian. "Wow, that's really neat. I was telling Sheila, one of the other consultants from work, how my granddaughter and adopted granddaughter are in a heavy metal band," she went on in an impressed, upturned tone, "and she said she'd like to come to one of your concerts sometime. If I can get her the details soon, maybe she can make it to the next one."

"We actually play something more like '90s alternative rock combined with punk and post-hardcore," I said.

"Oh. Well at any rate, write down the time and place of your show for me before you leave in the morning so I won't forget," said Grandma Vivian. "Now, what's the name of the other girl in your band again?"

"Gabby," I said.

Bern and I met Gabby Golubski in our music class freshman year. She was affable and non-judgmental with cool-brown hair and warm honey eyes. I liked her right away.

We began rehearsing in Gabby's basement since it was more feasible for Bern and me to transport guitars and amps back and forth than for Gabby to transport her kit. Her parents soon starting letting us keep our amps and my PA system set up there permanently so that it was easier to get practice going.

Gabby's basement was unlike our basements of old, second-string televisions and mismatched furniture, which was serviceable, but banished from our living rooms for its raggedness caused by years of jumping, rollicking children and dogs, condemned to hold laundry that needed folding. Hers was equipped with a giant wall-mounted TV, a fresh leather sofa and recliner set, and an arcade. The arcade included several pinball machines, Skee-Ball, foosball, the hoop game with the mini basketballs, and an air hockey table, which was used more for beer pong than for air hockey until they also got a beer pong table. There was a fully-stocked bar and the latest edition of pretty much every game console in existence downstairs as well.

The Golubskis lived in a cookie-cutter house in a Cleveland suburb called Westlake. Their Dave & Buster's-esque basement was only the start of its entertaining magnificence. They had an in-ground pool in the backyard, complete with a water slide and diving board, a deck with a fancy steel fire pit, a double grill, a hot tub, and a screened gazebo with another fire pit, a stone grill, and a bar. Naturally, their house was a party house.

Mr. Golubski was a CFO for some big metal manufacturing company and frequently went away on business. He set up trust funds for Gabby and her older sister. I didn't know what a trust fund was until

Gabby explained it to me. Mrs. Golubski was a stay-at-home mom.

When Mr. Golubski was in town for the weekend, there was almost always a family party, and if the party was on a day that Ardis Alchemy had practice, Bernadette and I were invited to stick around for it. When Mr. Golubski was out of town for the weekend, there was almost always a house party with a mix of Gabby's friends and her sister's friends. Gabby's mom seemed to instigate the house parties. She was an unauthoritative friend type of parent, but she always made sure anyone who drank stayed the night.

"Are either of you thinking about studying music in college?" Grandpa Adrian asked.

"I haven't put much thought into what to go to college for yet," Bernadette replied, tilting her head to the side, "but I know I want it to be something that will help me get a really good-paying job."

"Sure, sure," said my grandpa, looking down into his mug of still-steaming coffee. He brought it up near his mouth. "Nothing wrong with that," he added, and he took a careful sip.

"Since college is so expensive," Bern continued, "I feel like it's a necessity for me to go into a higher-paying field. My cousin is a teacher, and she barely makes enough to pay her student loans on top of her regular bills, which is crazy when you consider the fact that a degree is a requirement for teaching. It seems like careers that require college should earn you enough to afford your student loans, or that the employer should help pay them. To keep her loan payments low, she has to spread them out over a longer period of time, so really, she's paying even more in the long run with the interest." She drew in a big breath and exhaled with a sigh. "You know, sometimes I think college should be free. I hear it is in parts of Europe."

"That's true," said Grandpa Adrian, "but fewer people go to universities in those places. In Germany, for example, there's more emphasis on vocational schools and apprenticeships. The requirements to get into universities are different, and harder, than they are here. And the income tax is higher. Plus, they don't have all the fancy little liberal arts colleges. Universities are big and standardized. I'd imagine that to make them free here, at least public ones, we'd have to raise *our* income tax, or colleges would have to be more selective to keep enrollment down so that the costs to taxpayers wouldn't get out of control. Or, they'd have to make cuts to their programs and facilities. Maybe ..." he trailed off, folding his hands over the top of his coffee mug, "no dorms, no dining halls, no extracurriculars, fewer degree tracks." He shrugged.

"Yeah, that's possible," Bernadette said, slowly and thoughtfully nodding her head while shifting her eyes from side to side, like they were following her thoughts as they flip-flopped between the different angles of the conversation. She and I enjoyed these complex, multisided discussions that we often had with my grandfather.

"But who knows?" said Grandpa Adrian. "Maybe someone will find a better way to do it someday."

"It might be one of them," said Grandma Vivian.

"It *might*," said Grandpa Adrian. "You girls are both smart. I bet you can get scholarships to help pay for college. Perhaps an academic scholarship, or even one for music or the arts. You know, I got a scholarship to play football. Truly, I did." My grandpa nodded, wide-eyed, as though he thought his statement would be unbelievable to us otherwise and we'd chalk it up to be one of his "tall tales," as my grandma called them.

By that age, I could decipher which of his stories were fictitious or exaggerated on my own, and I sensed that he was aware of this based on the sly, twinkly grin he'd give me after he told those kinds.

My favorite of his tall tales was the one about how he met my grandmother. In reality, they met at a yacht party held by a couple they were mutually friends with. Grandma Vivian was a work friend of the woman, and Grandpa Adrian knew the woman's husband from an Italian-American club. They hit it off at the party and then kept finding themselves at the same social gatherings, which eventually led them to dating.

Grandpa Adrian gave me his version of how he and my grandma met on our way to what I called "the haunted park" at the end of their street. The haunted park had once been a school playground. It was maintained to serve as a neighborhood park after the school it sat in front of closed. The auditorium inside the school building became a hall for community events.

In my opinion, as a kid who'd just started kindergarten, the eerie vacantness of the classrooms meant they were haunted, and I was sure the ghosts who haunted the classrooms also haunted the playground.

"I attended a party one evening on a friend's boat down at the marina just over there on Lake Erie," his story started. He pointed in the general direction of the Edgewater Marina in Cleveland, which wasn't far from their house in Lakewood, as we walked along. "It was warm and pleasant out—the middle of summer," he went on. "Everyone was having fun, and then this woman who was probably having too much fun fell over the side of the boat into the water. She started splashing and yelling, trying to get back to the boat, and she caught the attention of a shark. He was a big one! He swam right up behind her, so I dove in to rescue her. I got her back onto the boat just in time. And then, as I was still holding her there on the deck, I looked into her eyes, and I said, by golly, this is the most beautiful woman I've ever seen. I'm going to marry her one day."

I didn't learn until the next summer, on a day my mom took my brothers and me to the beach, that there are no sharks in Lake Erie.

"Dani, why don't you want to go play by the water?" my mother asked. "I thought you liked playing by the water and making your mud pies." I wouldn't leave the blanket she was lying on to sun tan.

"I'm afraid a shark might get me," I said somberly.

"What?" my mom said with this scrunched-up face, like she'd tasted something bitter. "Dani, there are no sharks in the lake."

"Grandpa Adrian said one tried to eat Grandma," I replied.

"Oh, Dani, don't believe your grandpa. He was telling you a story," said my mom.

"So I heard your grandpa told you a shark tried to get me in Lake Erie," Grandma Vivian said to me the next time I was over. I nodded gravely, sitting at the kitchen table between my oldest brother, Andy, and my brother born after me, Patrick. Grandpa Adrian was seated beside our youngest brother, Mikey, who was still in a high chair, buttering slices of toasted Carmin's bread for us.

"That was just one of Grandpa's tall tales, honey. There aren't any sharks in the lake. Nothing is going to hurt you at the beach," my grandma said.

"Did I say it was a shark that tried to get your grandma?" said Grandpa Adrian. "I misspoke. It was a giant sturgeon. Almost swallowed her right up!"

"Oh, stop it, Adrian!" said Grandma Vivian. She shook her head at him and tsked. Then, still shaking her head, her look of disdain softened to an incredulous smile, and she laughed.

"You know," I said to my grandparents and Bernadette, "I am actually considering studying music. I'm considering a lot of things though."

My problem was never that I didn't know what I wanted to do; it was that I wanted to do so many things, and it didn't seem possible to do them all. But I thought I could be anything I set my mind to being, and I hoped to change the world in some way.

I could see myself as a recording engineer, gigging out of town with my band between studio projects, taking off whenever for DIY tours. I could see myself as an investigative or political journalist, an urban planner, a sailor in the Navy. I'd even dreamed of being president. I proudly declared to my fourth-grade teacher that I *would* one day be President of the United States of America, standing all stately and perfect-postured before her, the goody-goody, punish-myself-by-skipping-dinner-if-I-got-less-than-an-A-minus-on-a-test kid I was. She asked if I'd hire her to clean the White House after I moved in, and I said, "Absolutely."

"Well, there's plenty of time yet to make up your mind about what to major in," Grandma Vivian said. "You still have half of high school to go."

"I know," I said.

"You have lots to look forward to about college though," said Grandpa Adrian. "College was a wonderful time for me … with football and my fraternity …"

His gaze drifted up and away into the crystal chandelier above the table.

"I had to take some time off when I got drafted for Korea," my grandpa said, "but I returned to school right after my tour."

He took a fuller, less cautionary sip of the cooling coffee.

"What did you do in the military?" asked Bernadette.

"I was a typist."

"A typist?" said Bernadette, sounding perplexed.

"Yes, ma'am. Someone had to do it, and I was good at it because of college. There's more to the military than crawling through the mud and shooting rifles. Lots of other jobs need to be filled to keep the military running. I still did my part in taking out the enemy. Threw my typewriter at them."

"Oh, Adrian, you're so full of shit," said Grandma Vivian, laughing, and the rest of us laughed too.

THREE

After our late-night meal, the four of us went upstairs for bed. Bern and I had a designated room at my grandparents' house, which had been my mother's. It was painted peach, so we called it The Peach Room. We shared the queen bed in it. My grandma always made up the bed with starchy, white sheets and a flowery comforter, pulled tightly over two stacks of pillows and tucked under the mattress. The walls were decorated with framed Deco pieces and glass cases of expensive perfume that Grandma Vivian had gotten many years ago when she was an executive for an upscale department store chain. She'd been working with another company as a business consultant since the department store closed.

I never understood how, but Grandma Vivian continued accumulating hundreds of department store makeup and perfume samples. I could only guess an old friend of hers from the cosmetics industry kept sending them. She stashed the samples in a dresser in The Peach Room and in the hallway linen closet.

When I was little, she let my cousins and me use the makeup samples to play beauty salon. We'd give makeovers to each other and any family members who would come upstairs to our imaginary shop.

My grandma let us dress up in her pre-tunic-and-leggings-look clothes too. She stored them in The Peach Room's closet. There were swanky silk gowns, fur coats and stoles, designer suits, pointed-toe pumps, and go-go boots. I used to love twirling around in her gowns, which hung loosely off my body and fell into piles of fabric at my feet, while wearing my not-for-individual-sale makeup, feeling positively stunning. I'd pretend I was in some earlier, elegant era, heading out to one of the places Grandma Vivian had worn the gowns to—a cocktail party downtown, a casino, dinner on the rooftop of the Ritz-Carlton—in a black Cadillac with black leather interior, Dean Martin's voice emanating from the stereo, a handsome gentleman in a suit beside me.

Grandma Vivian would insist that Bernadette and I take home gift bags of her samples with other pretty little things thrown in that she'd buy us on impulse, like purses, jewelry, hair accessories, scented lotions, nail polishes, compacts, and stationeries. I discovered my signature lipstick shades in her goodie bags—true red and plum.

Bernadette decided to take a shower before she went to sleep. I decided I'd take one in the morning. As soon as she shut herself in the bathroom, I plopped belly-down on the middle of the bed and called Desmond.

"Hullo?" he answered.

"Hey, it's Dani."

"Hey! I didn't think you were going to call."

"Sorry. I know it's getting late. We were hanging out with my grandma and grandpa." I was so jittery that I couldn't be still. I sat up and crossed my legs.

"It's OK. It's really not that late," Desmond said. "I'm kickin' it at my buddy Eric's with Tommy and some other guys."

"Oh. Sounds fun," I said. I could hear boys' voices in the background.

"This is probably not the best place to talk actually—hard to hear. But I wanted to ask you—would you like to get pizza with me next week? I know a really good place. And maybe we can go bowling afterward?"

"Sure. I'd love that," I said.

"OK. Great. I'll call you tomorrow and we'll figure out a day and time."

"That works for me. Have a good night."

"All right. You too, Dani. Nice hearing from you. Bye."

I tapped the end button and heaved myself back onto a stack of pillows, thrilled and wanting more, slightly jealous of the other people and things holding Desmond's attention.

I turned the volume on my phone up higher than usual and placed it beneath my pillow in case Desmond texted after I'd fallen asleep. He did, to inform me that he was in the waiting room of an ER with Eric and would likely be there the rest of the night. Eric's oldest brother, a half-brother, Louis, had overdosed on heroin. He would survive, astonishingly. I've heard that almost never happens with heroin.

Louis had two tears tattooed below his right eye. He'd gotten them for a neighborhood gang he used to be in, according to Desmond. Once I stopped being too intimidated to really look at his face rather than only look at the gang markings on it, I noticed his eyes were softer than his brothers,' and sort of sad looking.

On our first date at the pizza shop, I told Desmond how sorry I was to hear about his friend and that he had to go through all that at the hospital.

He said, "Thanks. Yeah, it was horrible. I'll never fuck with needles."

"I'd sure hope not," I said, baffled that it wouldn't go without saying.

I disliked Eric from the day I met him. Every other weekend, he stayed in the upper unit of a Lakewood duplex with his father, step-mom, and brothers. I walked there with Desmond that day.

Desmond entered their half of the house without ringing or knocking. I followed him to a dim loft furnished like a living room. All the boys who hung around there called it "The Attic," like it was a venue or something.

Eric was sitting on a couch with a bong in his lap. On a loveseat sat two more guys, too engrossed in their video game to notice that Desmond and I were standing at the top of the stairs.

"Ey, Desmond!" said Eric, squinting at us. He set the bong down on the floor and stood up. I followed Desmond over to him.

Eric coughed into the crook of his arm and then gave Desmond a bro hug.

"This is Dani," Desmond said to him, placing his hand on the small of my back.

"Dani! Pleased to finally meet you. I'm Eric," he replied, touching my shoulder. "Desmond has told me lots about you."

Eric always spoke to me with a warmth so seemingly genuine that I could understand how the girls he went out with might actually believe he cared about them. His strawberry-blond hair had a sharp side part line. He wore dark-blue jeans and a plain-white tee with rolled-up sleeves. I thought he looked like a greaser. A handsome one at that.

Desmond and I sat on the couch, and Eric offered us the bong. Desmond took a hit, then tried handing it back to him.

"I'm done, man. You can keep it," Eric said. Still standing, he pulled a pack of cigarettes out of his pocket and lit one.

"You don't smoke, Dani?" asked Eric.

"Not really," I answered. I'd smoked weed a few times with Desmond. One time, I giggled a lot. The other times, I had anxiety and heart palpitations, so I decided I'd just stick to social drinking.

"Not cigarettes either?" said Eric.

"Nope," I said. I smoked a cigarette from Gabby's sister at a party of theirs once just to say I tried it, but I never had a real inclination to smoke cigarettes.

"Hey, that's cool," said Eric. "I'm sorry if my smoking is bothering you. I'll give you some more space." He stepped backward toward the stairs, reducing the potency of the cigarette smell. Then, he yelled, "Marc, when's that bitch gonna get here?"

"I dunno, dude," said Marc from the loveseat. "I told you she said she might not come over."

Marc was Eric's other older brother, and the one who hung around the most.

Eric put the butt of his cigarette in an ash tray on the coffee table in front of the couch. He said, "Aw, Desmond, you shoulda seen it last week," shaking his head. "You wouldn't believe this ho." He made eye contact with me as if to include me in the conversation.

"This girl I'd been seeing came over looking for me last Friday night, because I told her I'd probably get here around 8, but I ended up having to help my ma with some stuff and didn't come until Saturday. So she told Marc she'd just hang out and wait for me and winds up bangin' him. Then Louis comes home, and she goes and hangs out in his room with him. He didn't know about her and Marc, and she ends up sucking his dick!"

"Damn," said Desmond.

"Yeah, so when I show up, Marc goes, 'Oh, your girl came over for you last night, but uh, I fucked her, and I think Louis might have too.' So I'm like, what?" He re-enacted his jaw dropping. "I text her, you hooked up with my brothers, you nasty bitch? What's wrong with you? She didn't say nothin.' I told Marc we should just run a train on her next time." He laughed.

Desmond looked at Eric with his eyes real wide and his lips pressed together, appearing more astounded than amused. I could feel my face turning red-hot from the repulsion blazing in my gut.

"But nah, I don't fuck with her anymore," Eric said. "I guess she's still talking to Marc though. Whatever."

Eric brought Desmond and me glasses of iced tea. I took a few sips from mine and set it on the coffee table. The tea was overly sweet and left a gritty coating on my teeth, like the kind that comes in a plastic gallon jug, which it probably did, I thought.

Eric took a folding chair from its resting place against the wall and set it up across from us. He dropped down into the chair with a sigh and stretched out his arms. "So I'll most likely be staying here at my dad's for the next couple weeks because I'm suspended from school again."

"What happened?" Desmond asked.

"Got in a fight with some punk-ass bitch. You know," said Eric.

"How'd it go down?"

"I was in the cafeteria," Eric started.

Desmond leaned forward on the couch, his eyes lit up. He had a strange affinity for altercations. He'd call up his friends after a fight and go on and on about it the way I would with one of my girl friends after hanging out with a boy I liked. I learned he was notorious for getting into fights and other trouble at school.

I wasn't in the mood for a fight story. I stared intensely at my sweating glass of iced tea like I was studying some speck-sized species of fish swimming around inside it, concentrating on blocking out my surroundings and becoming lost in a sea of my own thoughts.

Sometime later, I felt a nudge on my shoulder.

"Have you become a mute?" said Desmond.

"No," I said.

My bladder was pulsing with the tea that I'd emptied from the glass. I asked Desmond if he could show me where the bathroom was. He led me downstairs to it and then went back up to The Attic.

After I finished using the bathroom, I moseyed around the living room, as I was in no great hurry to return upstairs, and nobody else was home anyway.

All the living room walls were painted a pure white. The sunlight coming in through the sheer window treatments reflected brightly off the white paint and shiny wood floors. There was no clutter anywhere. The décor was minimalist and match-y.

On the mantel were some framed photos. I noticed the one in the center first. It was of a middle-aged man and a middle-aged woman on a beach. The man had his arms wrapped around the woman. Obviously Eric's father and step-mother, I thought. A lot of parents I knew had similar photographs displayed in their houses, from vacations and whatnot. I supposed Eric's step-mother had decorated the living room.

Another one of the photos was of Eric, Marc, and Louis. They were younger, sitting side-by-side with their arms around each other's shoulders, and judging by the marshmallow skewer in Marc's hand, by a campfire. They all wore toothy, cheesy, kid grins. There was a picture like this of my brothers and me in a collage frame that hung in our living room from back when my parents would take us camping.

Next to the campfire picture was a fairly-recent-looking one of Eric, his older brothers, and a younger boy, who I guessed was their step-brother. Desmond had mentioned to me that their step-mom had a son from a previous marriage. They were standing in front of a Christmas tree, all in sweaters and blue jeans, with wrapped presents around their feet.

Feeling I had nothing left to look at, I finally went upstairs. As I made my way toward the couch, I saw that Desmond was nearly face-down on the coffee table. I thought he was keeling over, so I rushed toward him, but then, he lifted his head, taking in a breath really hard through his nose. There was a white, powdery residue on the table. He noticed me, and I could tell by his expression that I wasn't meant to witness what I had.

"Come here, babe," Desmond said, rubbing his hand in a circular motion on the couch cushion beside him. I sat.

"What took you so long? I missed you," he said, batting his eyelashes at me in a silly, childish manner.

"Really?" I huffed. My anger over the situation at hand and the whole miserable experience of being Desmond's appendage in what I thought was the most repugnant company I'd ever had the displeasure to meet was erupting. "Because you look like you've been pretty pre-occupied up here with your cocaine."

Desmond burst out laughing. "It's not cocaine, Dani," he said.

"Oh. Well what is it then?"

"Don't you worry about it," he answered in a smooth, calm voice before gently kissing my hairline, as if that would make the question simply simmer away.

I pulled away from him. "Tell me."

"All right. It's OxyContin. But I may have tried cocaine once or twice." He shifted his eyes from side to side and contorted his mouth in this stupid, smirky way, so I didn't know what to believe. Then he looked at me hazily and pulled me back into the couch to make out. I had to put my hands on his face to subdue the force of his tongue, which lurched down my throat like a snake going after its prey.

"You know, if you guys want a room, you can use mine and Marc's downstairs," said Eric. "Just make sure you pull the door in all the way, because it sticks and won't close completely, and my step-brother should be getting in from his dad's in a little bit. He'll try to sneak a peek. I don't think that little weasel gets laid yet."

Desmond turned to me and asked with his eyes if I wanted to move to the bedroom. I shook my head no.

"I think we're actually gonna be headin' out, brah," he said to Eric, standing up from the couch.

"Oh, for sure, man," said Eric. They gave each other another bro hug. "Come by again soon, aight? You too, Dani."

"Yeah," I said. I tried to force a smile, but I felt it come out as more of a grimace, so I shifted my eyes to the floor.

"So, I don't think I care to go to Eric's with you again," I said to Desmond once we started walking back to his house. "I mean, the way he talked about that girl was just awful. I really don't understand why you're friends with him."

"First of all, she's not exactly a classy girl," Desmond said.

"But he acts like he and his brothers are better than her—like she was the only one to blame for the love triangle they got into, er, square, I guess."

"Well, second of all, Eric is a brother to me, Dani. We've been friends since we were young kids, and we've been through a lot together. At the end of the day, he still has my back, and that's what's really important, so what do I care who or what he does? I don't concern myself with his sex life, so neither should you."

"Then no one should concern themselves with her sex life either," I muttered.

Desmond stepped in front of me and took me into his arms. "Hey, I promise Eric will never show you any disrespect," he said. "That would be disrespecting me, because you're my girl. And just because he acts a certain way doesn't mean I would. I like good girls, and there's only one good girl I want: you."

"OK," I said, realizing there were no other points I could make on the subject that would matter to Desmond.

He kissed my lips tenderly and we continued on our way.

FOUR

I looked OxyContin up online later at home after everyone else had gone to bed. I was sure to delete the browsing history in case my parents saw it and read too much into it. I guess I wanted to learn about it out of worry that Desmond would think I knew nothing besides what is along the straight and narrow path, making me capable of only straight and narrow thought or something, and for this reason, I was embarrassed to ask him what it is, hence my turning to the internet for the answer.

Desmond had the excellent ability to never get embarrassed. I recall only one time ever that I saw embarrassment on his face.

He needed to pick up tickets from a booking agent downtown, and I tagged along. Feeling nostalgic for an ice cream stand in his old neighborhood not too far from the booking agent's office, Desmond decided we'd stop there afterward.

"We're getting close," he said, just as a sign informed us that we were entering Midtown. The area was mostly barren lots, dotted with the quivering ruins of Victorian mansions and graffiti-scrawled, red-brick storefronts. I tried to picture this place in its prime: Shops were compacted all around the deserted, defaced ones remaining, and there was a constant influx of patrons wearing early-twentieth-century styles. Vibrantly-painted Victorian homes stood in perfect rows on the downward-sloping side streets, which, at a passing glance from the main road, looked like a swirl of watercolor paints, a spin of a lit-up carousel.

After a few more blocks, we pulled into a torn-up asphalt parking lot behind a factory with clouded-over windows. On the corner across the street stood a little white building with a red-and-white-striped awning. We made our way there and got in line behind two unchaperoned boys who couldn't have been more than 10 years old.

Adhered to the white walls were the typical faded, retro sundae and cone signs and two dry erase boards, which displayed the menu in teacher-looking handwriting with an assortment of brightly-colored markers.

Desmond got a large cone with vanilla and chocolate swirled that looked like the Leaning Tower of Pisa, and I got a small peanut butter one.

We sat down to eat on a bench near the sidewalk. Desmond painstakingly slurped up the bowing side of his twist to prevent it from toppling over, but it did anyway.

"Ah, motherfucker!" he shouted at the ground. We got stares from the two boys, who were sitting on another bench.

"I saw that coming," I said.

"Oh well," he shrugged. "Can I try some of yours?"

I handed him my cone.

"Mmm, yours is really good too. You know," he added, cocking his head and squinting off into the distance, "I kind of want to go up to my old house, just because."

"That's fine by me," I said. "It's really close to here, right?"

"Oh yeah, only a few streets down that way," he said, nodding ahead of us.

"Are we going to walk there?" I asked.

"No," he replied, his eyebrows lowered in concern. "You shouldn't be walking around this neighborhood. I don't wanna have to fight anyone today."

So after we finished our ice cream, we drove to Desmond's old street. All the way at the end of it, we stopped before a yellow house enclosed by a white picket fence. Some of the paint on the siding was starting to peel, but overall, the exterior of the home was decently maintained. There was a tidy flower garden in front of it.

"So that's it?" I asked Desmond, pressing my index finger over top of the yellow house from the inside of the car window.

"Not the yellow house," said Desmond. "The mother-in-law suite behind it."

I'd paid little notice to the structure sitting behind the house outside of the fence, having automatically assumed it was a storage shed.

"Oh, wow. It looks more like the clubhouse my dad built for us than a real house," I said.

"We couldn't afford much when my dad was in prison, and we didn't have anybody to stay with," said Desmond.

I turned to him. He was squinting through the windshield, and I could see the injury and humiliation in his eyes. He wouldn't break his gaze though I was certain he felt me staring at him. I had the same shame I did as a young child after my mother taught me how tactless it is to comment to someone on a physical imperfection of theirs.

"I'm sorry. That came out wrong," I said.

I'd always embarrassed easily, and when I did, I'd get even more embarrassed knowing that people could tell I was. My face never failed to give me away—the ruddiness in my cheeks and forehead, the beads of sweat that formed along my hairline and upper lip. Some things that made me feel stupidest were flubbing a guitar part or singing off pitch in front of an audience, being at a party where all anyone else wanted to do was dance to music from the hits station, misspelling, mispronouncing, or misusing words, and being completely ignorant of something mentioned in conversation, like OxyContin.

After a minute of silence, Desmond said, still unable to look at me, "The old lady who lives in the yellow house, or, well, *did* live in the yellow house—she could be dead for all I know—she used to watch us when my mom was at work because our babysitter turned out to be running a meth lab with her boyfriend. My mom was always working, and selling plasma, but it was never enough money to put us all in a real daycare. The lady kind of had a hard time keeping up with us given her age, but she didn't charge my mom—just asked her to mow her lawn sometimes—and she wasn't running no meth lab or nothin'. She was actually real nice. Fed us lots of stale graham crackers and Cheerios." He cracked a smile.

"Do you want to go knock on the door and see if she's still here?" I asked.

"No, I'd rather not," Desmond answered. "After my dad got out of prison, we moved to a bigger house two blocks away from here—one that wasn't in someone's backyard. I have fonder memories of this house though. I think I'd be fine if I never saw the other house again."

"How come?" I asked.

"My dad still drank heavily for a while after he came home. Living here was peaceful in comparison to living with him."

"Oh. Got it." I said.

"Yeah, well, that's enough of that," Desmond said, slapping the lower part of the steering wheel. "Let's get out of here."

Desmond's dad, Ron, served three years in a state penitentiary for severely injuring another guy in a bar fight, resulting in brain damage. He was a serial burglar before that, but authorities were never able to nail him for it. While in prison, Ron met Eric's dad. They decided to arrange a play date for their sons when they were both released, which is how Desmond and Eric's friendship started.

According to Desmond, Ron had also gotten away with killing someone. He told Desmond a man with a knife had attacked him in an alley behind a bar, so he strangled him with an old extension cord that was hanging out of a dumpster. He didn't go to the police out of fear they wouldn't believe it was self-defense. Instead, he drove into the alley, stuffed the guy's body in his trunk, then went and dumped it on the tracks in a secluded area to be pulverized by a train so that the death would be ruled as an accident if anyone found the remains. He said he never heard of anyone looking for the dead guy though, probably because he'd been such a low life that nobody cared he was missing. That story always haunted me.

It was after Ron broke Desmond's arm and Mandy, Desmond's mom, separated from him for it that Ron quit drinking. Desmond was riding his bike in the driveway, and Ron picked up the bike, Desmond still on the seat, and threw them both. Desmond said Ron's corporal punishment was always more like abuse before he was sober, and he was physically and verbally abusive to Mandy.

Mandy was exceptionally warm and giving to those she liked, and she ended up liking me very much, but I could tell she was skeptical in the beginning. She didn't say any more than hello the first time I came over, and I felt the pin pricking of judgement on my skin as she looked me up and down in my St. Ambrose uniform.

One day, Desmond told me he had to make a stop at Eric's on his way home from school and that if he wasn't back by the time I arrived to hang out, his mom would let me in the house. I was hoping that wouldn't be the case to spare me the discomfort of being alone with an adult who I didn't really know and didn't think liked me.

Mandy answered the door. "Hi, Dani. Desmond isn't here yet, but you can come in and wait for him." *Of course*, I thought.

When I went inside, she said, "I'm heating water for tea. Do you like tea, hon?"

I told her yes.

"Why don't you come into the kitchen with me and pick out what kind you'd like to drink. I have so many."

Most of Mandy's teas were for home remedies. She kept lots of herbs and oils around for therapeutic purposes too. She had chronic pain from a work accident, which had required multiple spinal surgeries so that she could even walk again, and heavy pain meds for a while. She developed an addiction to the meds. Once she got clean, she started using medicinal marijuana and all these other alternative therapies for pain management, and then she swore by them for basically everything.

I decided on mint green tea.

"We can take these into the living room," said Mandy after pouring the boiling water into our mugs. "I've been watching TV while dinner cooks."

I sat next to Mandy on the couch. She picked up the remote and lowered the volume of the television.

"So," she said as she put the remote down. I turned to her, anticipating a question to follow. She just looked at me, deeply and inquisitively, the corners of her mouth slightly upturned, like she was solving a riddle inscribed across my face.

She then picked up her mug and dunked her tea bag several times. "You know, I can see my son is really into you, and that's saying a lot, because he's very picky when it comes to girls. I predict you'll be around for a while."

I had no idea there was so much to be particular about in regard to the physical features of a potential partner until I started seeing Desmond. Before him, I don't recall having much awareness of my own physical features, aside from my hair and height, because I got made fun of for them. I was comfortable and confident with the rest of my attributes as they were without being totally conscious of *how* they were, and I didn't often compare myself to other girls.

Desmond reminded me regularly what he liked about my appearance, as I'm sure anyone could appreciate from their partner. Hearing I met the specifications that made up his ideal beauty gave me assurance that he'd stay.

He'd tell me he loved that I'm curvy yet fit. I suppose I developed that way by a combination of genetics and playing sports. Bernadette said it was lucky that I have curves since my frame is small—that I'd easily get lost among people otherwise. I was shorter than average my whole life, like much of my family, topping out at only 4'11 on a good day.

I really never minded my height. I only minded that kids in grade school would storm me with short jokes that I felt I had to fake laugh at, and that in college, other students frequently asked if I'm a legal midget, if I get scholarship money for being a midget, and if I collect disability benefits from the government for legal midget status—and those questions weren't jokes. They were completely serious.

Desmond would also tell me how he loved my hazel eyes, porcelain skin, and curly brunette hair. I grew to love my hair too, but I was insecure about it in grade school because kids would always comment on how "poufy" it was, and the girls constantly asked why I didn't straighten it. I started wearing it to my lower back in high school to bring down its volume. These two idiot boys from Holy Rosary would stick little wads of paper in the back of my hair when they were sitting behind me, and this girl named Kathleen would sometimes come up to me at recess and tug on the short curls that fell in my face, then run away, laughing. She'd also whisper to other girls in the bathroom about my hair's general ugliness.

"The way I see you and Desmond look at each other reminds me of his father and myself when we were kids," said Mandy. "Desmond is a spitting image of his dad at that age."

"Really? Huh …" I said. I couldn't picture it. I had already seen Ron by this point. He was tall and kind of burly with a shaved head and a beard, and he was missing one of his front teeth. He wore earrings and a bandana. I noticed, because he'd been in a short-sleeved shirt, that he had several satanic tattoos on his arms. He also had a cross tattooed on each middle finger. Desmond explained that the finger tattoos meant "fuck God," like Ron was flipping off the crosses.

"Here, I'll show you some photos," Mandy said. She set her tea down on the side table and walked over to the TV stand, which had a built-in cabinet, and picked a couple albums out of it.

"These are really old." She opened an album between our laps on the couch. "Here's me and Ron at my freshman homecoming." They were standing under a balloon-covered archway. It was one of those professionally-taken photos that you can order.

"Wow, Ron did look a lot like Desmond then," I said.

"Yeah, that was back when he let his hair grow out. This is even older," said Mandy, pointing to a photo on the top of the next page of Ron cradling an infant. "That's our firstborn he's holding. I had him when I was *14!* Ron was 16."

"Desmond told me that actually," I said. I was still figuring out how to hide my utter shock at that fact when it was mentioned. I'd hardly done any kissing by 14, so making babies wasn't even a near possibility. The only things I thought about making at that age were music and As on my report cards.

"We had Desmond a couple years later, and then the twins were born three years after him. We got married right when I turned 18. I would've gotten married sooner, but my father wouldn't give consent. My mom passed away when I was seven, so my dad was all I had. He and my siblings weren't much help when the kids were young because they hated Ron. They try to talk to us more now. I guess they've gotten over all their shit with me, but I'm still not over all my shit with them, so I don't bring my family around them too much."

"I see," I said.

"Ron and I actually separated for a little bit. We almost got divorced."

"Desmond told me about that too."

"I've always been a fool for his dad, and I wanted him to have the chance to be around for the kids if he could get it together. One day, he finally cleaned up his act, so I forgave him, and now here we are …"

I flipped through the other photo album by myself after Mandy went to get dinner out of the oven. Suddenly, the front door opened, and in stepped Ron. He looked surprised to see me. I was really glad when Desmond walked in right behind him.

For a while, I was afraid of being alone in a room with Ron. I wouldn't go to the kitchen for a drink or pass through the living room to get my shoes from the door mat without Desmond if I knew Ron was there.

"Oh shit, we've got the baby pictures out already. Mom!" Desmond called with fake exasperation. He sat down next to me on the couch, put his arm around me, and kissed my cheek. "Sorry you had to wait," he said.

The first time I was alone with Ron was in the Carveys' driveway. I was getting music equipment out of my car because Desmond was going to help Ardis Alchemy record some demos. I heard Ron's gruff voice from over my shoulder—the gruffest voice ever—as if he smoked three packs a day and washed down his dinner each night with a glass of shrapnel. He said, "Here, sweetheart. Let me help you with that."

I thought, *sweetheart?* How inconceivable that a voice like that from a man like him could ever produce such a tender word!

Ron helped me with a lot of little things over the years. He repaired my car on several occasions and gave it regular maintenance checks for free. When I stayed over on a night that it snowed, he'd take the time to brush my car off in the morning and help dig it out if necessary. So strange, I'd think, how someone who gives me chills can also warm my heart with their kindness—how a good deed can make a person you'd considered bad seem redeemable. Everything I knew to be black and white blurred together into grayness, and reality started to have endless slants.

FIVE

I started at a local state university the fall following high school graduation. I didn't have much choice to go anyplace else. Our family fell into the bracket of the middle class that doesn't qualify for federal grants but also can't afford the costs of tuition, room, and board without assistance, and my parents weren't able to take out loans for us. They believed an all-or-nothing approach to providing for us was the fairest; that is, if they couldn't give something to each one of us, they wouldn't give it to any of us. I received an academic scholarship from the university, but it was only a partial one, so I took out the Subsidized Loan and Direct Unsubsidized Loan to cover the remaining tuition and commuted to school since those loans can't be used for room and board. Because the government considers any student dependent who is not at least 24 years old, married, a graduate or professional student, a veteran or member of the armed forces, an orphan, a ward of the court, someone with legal dependents other than a spouse, an emancipated minor, homeless, or at risk of becoming homeless, there was nothing I could do on my own to get additional federal aid.

I decided to major in Journalism and minor in Political Science.

Desmond didn't go away to college either. He got a full-time job as a construction laborer.

Between spotty attendance for skipping and suspensions, poor grades for not doing work, and all the time spent in the principal's office, the only college he would have been accepted to, if he'd bothered to apply to any, was a community college. I did most of his homework senior year to make sure he graduated.

Gabby wanted to stay close to home, so she went to the same university that I did. We would meet up between classes to get lunch, hang out in common areas, and explore downtown. As we were both still gung-ho about the band, we kept it going together.

Having Gabby around all the time made no longer having Bernadette around all the time sting less. Bernadette went to a university in Connecticut. The summer before freshman year, she looked up her roommates online so they could discuss who would bring what for their dorm, and every time she talked about them, my stomach dropped. I tried my best to show excitement for her, you know, be a good friend, but I was constantly reminded of the things I was going to miss out on by living off campus, and I admit, I was jealous of Bern's roommates. I kept imagining all the cool new experiences they'd get to have with her, my best friend, without me. I feared I was going to be replaced.

Fortunately, Gabby did live on campus, so she was able to keep me in the loop about social events happening outside of school. I went to my first college party with her, at a frat house.

"The house is really close by. We can walk there in no time," she said as she mixed bottom-shelf vodka with grape Gatorade in a plastic cup. We pre-gamed in her room with a few of her new friends.

"You can have this one, Dani," Gabby said, holding the cup out to me. "Let me know if it's not strong enough."

I brought the drink up to my mouth. The Gatorade hardly masked the rubbing-alcohol smell of the low-quality vodka. I threw it straight back into my throat so I wouldn't taste it.

I had a medium-sized purse containing some make-up and hair product with me in case I needed to touch anything up before we left the dorm. After another cup of the vodka mix, which I'd stopped minding the taste of so much by then, I went for my lip gloss.

"Oh, Dani, can we put these in your purse?" one of Gabby's friends asked. She had a can of Four Loko in each hand. The girl she showed up with was standing beside her with a can of Four Loko too. "We wanted to take these to the party, but we forgot to bring something to hide them in on the way there."

"Um, sure," I said. I didn't have the heart to say no and be a fun killer though I was paranoid about walking through the highly-patrolled area of town with a bulky, sloshing bag.

I could feel the slight chill of early fall in the air that night. My spine began to tingle with an overwhelming sense of familiarity as memories of back-to-school jitters, warm colors, warm beverages and clothes, and Halloween festivities flooded my mind. I breathed deeply, as to take in every hint of autumn crispness the breeze had to offer and savor it, knowing that a rekindled flame of consciousness goes out as quickly as the season.

The frat house was a bit farther than I'd expected it to be. I struggled to keep up with Gabby's brisk pace in my merlot pumps, which I'd bought with a little black dress especially for the occasion. My outfit cost me nearly half a paycheck from my part-time job at Target, but I felt it was worth shelling out my sparse bills for. Most of the clothes in my closet were over-worn and beginning to feel dowdy, and the rest of my clothes were never worn for good reasons.

Gabby was wearing dark-wash jeans with a few well-placed tears above the knees, a black chiffon blouse, and black flats. Her grown-out bangs were clipped back, and the rest of her hair fell around her shoulders in soft waves. She impressed me with how well she could make casual clothes and a simple hairstyle look dressed up.

I could smell the bonfire that crackled in the back-yard as soon as we reached the rickety front porch of the old frat. Our little group made our way to the fire to mingle. The bubbly people there with their bubbly drinks were all hellos and hugs and, "What's your major?" Everyone seemed like a potential good friend in the intoxication of the moment. We wandered back and forth between the outside and inside of the house, finding the next place to be after the energy around us expired. Gabby's friends gradually split off from us.

By the time Gabby was ready to leave, I felt pretty sobered up. She'd poured half of the Four Loko her friends gave her into a cup for me, and that was all I had to drink besides the vodka mix in her dorm, since I didn't have my own connection to an individual of age who was willing to buy me booze. I nursed the Four Loko to have something to hold and sip on as everybody around me did, which really just squandered the effect of the alcohol.

There were a bunch of bottles on the kitchen counter, and I had gone to see about them earlier. As I was checking out the selection, a lanky, dorky-looking kid—most likely one of the fraternity's pledges, I thought—came and towered over me. He said to me, with his hands on his hips, "That liquor isn't for the general public, but I may be able to hook you up if you show me your tits." He stood back and folded his arms as though giving me my cue to flash him.

"I don't want it that badly," I replied. The boy shrugged and turned his back. I wished I could pick up one of the bottles and hit him over his stupid, long head with it.

As Gabby and I were rounding up the girls we came with from the living room, a voice called, "Dani Moran?"

I searched the mob for someone I knew. A grin spread across his face when we locked eyes.

"Matt Weathers!" I said.

Matt had been one of Andy's Holy Rosary friends, and my favorite of them. I stopped seeing him around as much in high school, being busy with my own social life and all, and I completely lost track of him when he and my brother graduated.

"I didn't know you go to school here!" he said.

"I didn't know you go here either. It's been years."

"It has." He paused and gave me a once over. "So how are you?"

"I'm great," I said.

"Glad to hear it! We really need to catch up."

"That would be fantastic," I said, "but I'm actually on my way out. Can we maybe catch up after class sometime?"

"Absolutely. I'll buy you lunch," he said.

"Aw, that would be so nice of you."

"Let me get your number," he said. "I'll shoot you a text so you have mine, and we'll plan something for next week."

I gave him my number, and then our group walked back to the dorm. Everyone went their separate ways except for me, since I was the only one without a bed somewhere on campus. I had planned to crash on Gabby's couch.

I went into Gabby's bathroom and kicked off my shoes, peeled off the clingy, black dress, and scrubbed the makeup from my face. I put on the t-shirt and pajama pants that Gabby had given me to sleep in, and afterward, I wandered into the living room, where Gabby was spreading a blanket out on the couch for me below a pillow. She lived in a quad where she shared a bedroom and bathroom with one girl, and the living room, which contained a kitchenette, with all three of the other girls.

"Thanks for making my bed," I said.

"No problem. I'm getting the munchies. Want to have a snack after I get dressed?"

"Sure," I said.

As Gabby walked off to her room, I pulled my phone from my purse to see if Desmond had called or texted. I'd put it on vibrate, resolving not to be that person who obsessively checks their phone while out, and I'd stopped thinking about it at the party, being too consumed by exciting, unnerving newness. Turned out Desmond had called and texted a lot.

I read his first few messages.

"Hey Dani. Are you back yet?"

"Call me."

"Hello?!!"

"What the hell are you doing?! Pick up!!!"

His anger appeared to grow as the messages went on. I decided not to keep reading and deleted them all.

I'd started listening to one of the voicemails he left when Gabby came back from her room. Scared she might be able to hear Desmond's harsh words through the speaker in the silence that surrounded us, I spastically hit the end button and dropped my phone onto the couch like it was covered with ants.

"Everything all right?" Gabby asked.

"Yeah, I'm fine," I told her.

"Boy drama?"

"I guess you could say that. Desmond is apparently pretty mad that I haven't talked to him all night."

"Oh, I see," she said, smooshing her lips to the side of her face and squinting her eyes. She pulled a couple bags out of the freezer and held one up in each hand. "French toast sticks or tater tots?"

"Tough one," I said.

"Well, why not both?"

"Heck, why not?" I answered.

Gabby started spreading the French toast sticks and tots onto baking sheets.

"I think it's OK if you do your own thing sometimes," she said. "I wouldn't even call Desmond back tonight if it were me. I'd give him time to cool off. It might all blow over. Maybe just text to let him know you're safe in my dorm and that you'll call tomorrow, if it makes you feel better."

"Yeah, I'll do that. You're probably right," I said, feeling warm and consoled for the moment.

SIX

The first conscious thought I had when I awoke was that Desmond was still upset, and it sent a bolt of terror through me. I wondered if he was even worse than last night since I hadn't called yet. And how late did I sleep anyway? I was afraid to check the time and see more pissed-off messages and missed calls from him. I felt an urgency to go home.

I went into Gabby's bedroom and found her sitting cross-legged on her bed with her laptop. Her roommate appeared to be out.

"Well good morning!" she said, looking up from the screen. "How'd you sleep?"

"I slept well," I answered. "So it's still morning?"

"For another hour and a half, technically," she said "but the dining hall stops serving breakfast at 11, and I'm jonesing for some pancakes. Want to come eat with me? I have guest swipes on my meal card."

"Oh, thanks, but I'm good," I said. "I was actually going to head home."

"Going to go work things out with Desmond?" she asked.

"I hope so," I replied, feeling sort of pathetic for how obvious I was.

"Me too," she said.

Mikey and my parents were sitting in the living room with the TV on when I got in. My dad and Mikey were watching a show, and my mom was reading a book. I never understood how she was able to read right there in front of the television, especially with the volume turned way up, like it typically was. I found it nearly impossible to read or do homework near the TV. I had to shut myself in my bedroom to focus.

"Hi!" I called out hastily to the three of them with my head down as I ran upstairs to the bathroom. I felt like I was excreting booze and images of racy things people assume happen at frat parties, which I didn't want my family to think of me doing. I didn't want to be seen at all until I showered and could fix my face and hair and be rid of every remaining trace of the night before.

I was standing in my underwear, shaking off the towel turban I'd made to soak up the excess water that held so well in my heavy curls, when my doorknob started jiggling. I always locked the door so nobody would be able to enter my room at a discommodious time, such as when I was half-naked. Still, I clutched myself in slight panic as if I *could* be barged in on at any moment, realizing I had nothing in immediate reach to cover my butt cheeks, which were gleaming around a thin, black, lace thong, and the cleavage popping out from my black push-up bra with lacy, pink embellishments. Desmond particularly liked those pieces of my wardrobe. I'd texted him that I was going to come over after I went home and got ready.

"Who is it?" I said. But I knew it was my mother. She was the only person who indignantly rattled my doorknob as if in protest of having to knock—like it was such an offensive condition for access considering her entitlement to everything and anything in the house as the owner of it.

The knob on my bedroom door had once been the only in the house without a lock built into it. After much embarrassment and complaining to my family in my more self-conscious pubescent years about them recurrently walking in on me while dressing, my dad finally replaced the old doorknob with one I could lock for privacy—a concept I began to revere like a holy day because I felt I had so little of it.

"It's me," my mom answered. "Are you planning to be around for dinner?"

"No. I'm going over to Desmond's," I said.

"Oh." I could hear her sigh through the door, so I knew she hadn't so much been asking if I'd be around for dinner as she was requesting that I be.

"I'm making chicken parm tonight with Grandma's sauce. Just thought you might like to be home to eat and maybe help cook. I bought ice cream for dessert," she said.

"I'm sorry," I said. "Let me know in advance next time you plan to make something special."

"OK," she said with a huff of disappointment. The hallway creaked with her retreating footsteps, and I went to work on detangling my hair.

When I got to the Carveys,' Mandy let me inside. "Hi, hon," she said. "Desmond's downstairs."

The basement had become Desmond's bedroom. As I descended the basement steps, I found Desmond sitting on the couch, his guitar beside him, his dog, Lee, sleeping at his feet, and a bong resting on his knee. Desmond smoked more pot than any person I'd ever known. He smoked to sleep. He smoked to eat. He smoked to start his day. He smoked for fun. He smoked to relieve stress. He smoked just to smoke. He got his weed from Ron. After he caught Desmond smoking in the garage in middle school, Ron decided he'd rather supply him with pot from his own trusted dealer than let him meet up with potentially shady dealers and risk getting in trouble.

Lee awoke and leapt up to greet me, licking my hands and face, his tail wagging wildly. Desmond acted as if he hadn't even heard me come downstairs. I knelt to kiss Lee's nose and scratch the top of his head.

Lee was an English Bulldog. He had a meek, sad disposition—surprising, I thought, for a dog like that, all thick and strong. It didn't look right on him.

Ron got Lee from a friend when he was a puppy and surprised Desmond with him for his fifteenth birthday. Desmond and his sister, one of the twins, who was so adoring of Desmond and always trying to emulate him in every way, thought it would be hilarious to name him Fugly—Lee for short—because of his build, wrinkly skin, and underbite.

The desire for a dog was a fleeting one for Desmond. He got over Lee the way a girl gets over Barbies. He couldn't be bothered with him anymore—tolerated him at most. He wasn't exactly an animal person.

If I gave Lee attention while Desmond was talking to me, he'd look at me with annoyance, like, how dare I not give my full attention to him and what he was saying. Lee was overjoyed when I petted him, scratched behind his ears, or rubbed his belly. He'd start doing this bark that sounded like a seal's.

Mandy was the one who really took care of Lee; she fed him and groomed him and gave him affection when I wasn't there. To everyone else in the house, he was just a nuisance—a pile of shit sitting on their floor that they were all sick of having to see and smell and walk around to get from point A to point B.

One time, Desmond's sister was walking with a full laundry basket in front of her face and tripped over Lee. She spilled all the laundry, and then she kicked the crap out of him for it. He ran, whimpering, under the dining room table. She looked all pragmatic and cool when she began picking up the dropped clothes, like she believed what she'd done was a common dog training technique or something. It really disturbed me. I gave Lee an extra-long belly rub that day.

Lee started to hit Desmond's shin with his wiggling butt and do his seal bark. Desmond yelled at him to "go the fuck away," and Lee quickly circled behind my back.

"Hey, there's no reason for that," I calmly said to Desmond. He glanced at me finally but still said nothing.

I picked up his guitar and placed it in its stand. Then, I sat down next to him and put my hand on his shoulder. He pulled away.

"Desmond, come on," I said. "Let's stop this and just talk. Why does me going out with some friends have to be such a problem for us? It was innocent. Really. And I mean, you go out with your friends all the time, and I never say anything about it."

"It's different," he said.

"How is it different?"

"When I go out with my friends, I'm not hanging around a bunch of strangers. You probably had dudes coming up to you all night, and I bet you talked to all of them because you're naïve."

"I'm not naïve. And yes, I introduced myself to some guys, but I wasn't being flirtatious, and I definitely didn't think about cheating on you with any of them. I don't feel like I've ever done anything that should warrant you being so distrusting of me."

"Not anything I've found out about," he scoffed. "You could be sneaky, or a liar. Women are all liars."

"Wow," I said. "I know you don't really believe that. You're just emotional."

He didn't respond.

"Desmond, I'm not looking for anyone else," I said. "You know how much I love you. You can come to parties on campus with me if you want. I don't care. I just don't want to fight about this stuff."

Desmond stared off into space like he was deep in contemplation. I kept my gaze fixed on him in wonder of how well he could ignore my presence and out of curiosity of how long he could keep it up. He placed the bong on the floor and sat back into the couch, wrapping an arm around me.

"Can you *show* me how much you love me? I could use a reminder," he said, finally looking into my eyes with a hint of a smile.

I moved in closer to kiss him. For a moment, I paused, my lips parted, to take in his breath. The taste of his breath, his mouth, his skin appealed to me in a way that seemed innate and animalistic. So strange and even cruel how attraction works by these unconscious, chemical means.

Desmond bit into my bottom lip and held it between both of his. When he released it, our tongues crashed together. I pulled and wound his hair with my fingers as we made out. His hands were pressed tightly to my face. Then he grabbed my hips, and I climbed onto his lap.

He unknotted my flannel shirt, and I helped him take it off. He gently touched my throat, ran his hand down slowly, and brushed his fingertips across the top of my breast. I started undoing his pants, and he reached into the cup of my bra.

I heard someone walking toward the basement door off the kitchen. I froze, afraid they were about to burst through it. Desmond's family occasionally caught us off us guard when they came downstairs to use the washer or dryer or to let the dog out, forcing us to frantically button and zip ourselves back up or to run for cover in the corner of the smaller back room that was mostly shielded by the furnace and Desmond's disorderly dresser. It held clothes piled high upon notebooks, loose change, empty or mostly empty packs of cigarettes, and other miscellaneous items he'd removed from the pockets of his jeans. It was never safe to undress completely until everyone else had gone to sleep.

The only other way we could be intimate without his family catching us was to do it in some covert place outside, like a park, the woods, a stairwell to the basement of a building, an alleyway, one of our cars in an empty parking lot. But then, of course, you have to worry about other people catching you.

"Let's go to the bed so we're farther from the stairs in case someone comes down," said Desmond, taking my hand. His bed was also in the back room.

"I think you should get a little couch for back here too," I said to him. I plopped down onto the bed. "Or maybe a recliner."

"Oh yeah? Some sex furniture?" He laughed.

SEVEN

From then on, if I was invited to a party, I also invited Desmond. He almost never came along, but I thought, at least I asked. I attended events for Desmond's friends and acquaintances more than he attended any for mine. We mostly went to parties at his friend Bobby's house. He threw one about every other weekend. Desmond and Bobby went to high school together but didn't become friends until the end of it, so I didn't know Bobby before college. He lived in the upstairs of a Lakewood duplex with a roommate.

Bobby was a rapper. He did a show with other artists every few weeks at a place called The Rubber Mill, which had originally been a rubber factory. The stage was in a big open ground-level room next to some skate ramps. All the shows were DIY and BYOB.

The rest of The Rubber Mill was rented out as studio space. In high school, Ardis Alchemy made an album in a recording studio located on the third floor. It took us about a year to complete. We did three songs per session, using money we'd saved up from our jobs and paid music gigs to cover them.

During one of the sessions, we met a band from Slovakia that was also making an album. They'd been deceived by the studio's website, which boasted comfortable living quarters for out-of-town bands doing long projects. The living space was one cramped room with two thin, bare mattresses on bunk beds. The only bathroom you had access to was a squalid community bathroom down the hall from the studio with no showers, toilet paper, or paper towels. We ladies always came with our own toilet paper and sanitizing wipes.

One day, the drummer of the Slovakian band asked us, "Are you guys famous in America?" They were apparently pretty well known in their country and Central Europe, playing arena shows and what have you.

"Oh yes, we're very famous," Gabby said.

"Wow. It's so cool to be able to talk with a big American band," one of the other guys said. "Can we ask you a few questions for the documentary we're making? We want to remember everything about our first trip to America."

"Sure," I said. "But I hope you'll at least forget about the bathroom."

They filmed us telling our names and answering some questions about the album we were working on. Gabby and I would joke for years to come that if everything in our lives should go to shit, we could move together to a small country like Slovakia, where we could easily make a splash as musicians and become rich and famous.

So at Bobby's parties, it was always beer pong in the dining room and poker in the kitchen, and people would smoke and hang out in Bobby's bedroom. That's where he was, passing around some blunts with friends, when Desmond introduced me to him, and we stayed there so Desmond could smoke too.

"Desmond, how's the band been doing?" asked Bobby. When he wasn't at his job, Desmond was focused on his band and his solo project.

"It's doing great, man. Our show last weekend was sick. We opened for C City." C City was a Columbus band making a name for itself at the time. "Their manager loved our set and wants us to come on their next tour."

"Wow, that's fucking awesome," said Bobby.

I thought Desmond's recounting of the conversation was a bit of an exaggeration. I'd overheard it while sitting at the bar near where he and the manager were talking. Ardis Alchemy was also one of the openers. C City's manager told Desmond he thought their set was "pretty tight." It had sounded more to me like Desmond insisted his band be booked for their next tour than it was suggested with such enthusiasm by their manager, as Desmond's story would lead one to believe. Desmond had a habit of embellishing details, giving false grandeur to stuff he did and that happened to him, like he was living in a Hollywood movie.

"Let me know if you guys do get on that tour, man," said Bobby. "I'll definitely catch a show."

"For sure," Desmond said.

A girl across the room who'd gone to Desmond's high school had been looking at him longingly while he spoke, and now she was sizing me up. She broke her stare when I stared back. I caught another chick watching Desmond lustfully from the living room couch as we passed by. There was at least one girl like them at every party he brought me to.

Desmond leaned in to kiss me. "You look so good tonight," he told me.

We were sitting on the floor in the circle of smokers, and I had my knees tucked since I was wearing a denim skirt, with fishnet tights and boots. Desmond slid his hand under my skirt and grabbed my ass.

"I can't wait to get you out of these tights. I might have to clear this place out and do it now."

"Desmond," I said, sensing a slight awkwardness had descended on the room, and I brushed his hand away.

I was insulted that he hadn't mentioned my band played the C City show too as I was sitting right next to him. I realized the only things he ever did say about me had to do with physicality. On the surface, they were compliments: "You look so good tonight. I love your figure. Your hair is beautiful." But deep down, I think he liked putting me on display to call more attention to himself and boost his ego. He needed to be the star in every movie-scene moment of his life and always cast me as the overly-sexualized female supporting character who's only there to rally around the male lead or be his trophy in the end.

I wished Desmond would talk about me the way Matt Weathers talked about his girlfriend. Her name was Emily Fairchild. She went to a small private college a couple hours away. She studied Physical Therapy, had one older sister, liked to paint, wanted to buy a horse and move to a quaint and quiet town close enough to

Cleveland that she wouldn't have a painfully-long work commute to one of the world's finest hospitals, and she really missed her cat, Mitten, who lived at home with her mom since she couldn't bring him to college. She was the salutatorian of her high school class and top in her Physical Therapy program. Well, she and another girl were always going back and forth between the first and second spots, but Matt had full faith that she'd graduate valedictorian this time.

If I wasn't with Gabby between my classes, I was usually with Matt. He helped me figure out a lot of school-related things, like how to select courses that fulfilled multiple degree requirements, how to navigate campus, and where to find parking. He was also a dependable band supporter. He came to almost all our shows. Sometimes he brought Emily.

We were back into shows after just a month of practicing with the new bassist, Layla. Our first show together was at Flanders', which happened to be right across the street from the university, so of course, Matt was there, along with a bunch of other people we knew from school.

I hung out at the bar with Matt before our set.

"Where's Desmond tonight?" he asked, reaching for the frosty glass of beer that the bartender had just given him.

"His band has a show too," I said. I was secretly relieved that they did, as I was nervous Desmond would be rude to Matt due to his tendency to get jealous.

"We're going to Kalahari next week for my birthday," I said, surprising myself with how defensive my tone was.

"Oh, it's your birthday next week? What day?" said Matt.

"Thursday. I'm excited to go someplace where we can swim and be warm this time of year without having to travel."

"Yeah, I hope it's a good time for you guys. So Thursday—I'll remember that," he said.

And he did. We'd agreed to meet in the Student Center during common hour that day and then go get lunch. The Student Center was particularly crowded because several organizations were holding fundraisers. Matt greeted me with a big smile, a hug, and a "happy birthday." Then, he handed me a small box. "Student Council was selling these, so I picked some up for you since it's your special day," he said. They were chocolate-covered strawberries.

"Oh my gosh, thank you so much! That's so sweet of you," I said to him.

I went to Desmond's after school. We weren't planning to leave for Kalahari until Saturday morning, but Desmond wanted to give me my birthday gift that evening and cook me dinner.

When I went downstairs, Desmond was studying soundwaves on his Mac monitor. I could hear drums and guitar blaring through his headphones. Trying not to startle him, I gently placed my hand on his shoulder.

He pulled his headphones down off his ears, letting them hang around his neck, and spun around in his wheeled desk chair. He put his hand on my hip and softly rubbed it. He looked somber. I hugged him to my chest and kissed his head.

"You OK?" I asked.

"Yeah, I'm fine." he sighed, not sounding so convincing.

I took off my coat and stuffed my scarf and gloves into one of its sleeves. I placed the coat on top of my tote bag by the stairs and sat down on the couch.

Desmond closed the recording program and walked into the back room. He came out with two wrapped presents. "Happy birthday, babe," he said to me, placing them next to me. He got me a chorus pedal and a pretty, baby-blue picture frame, which he'd already put my favorite photo of us in.

Desmond took a bag of weed from an old cigar box that sat among some other little boxes and trinkets on a wall shelf beside the computer desk. As he began pushing the weed into a grinder, my stomach reminded me it had been a long time since lunch. I remembered I had the strawberries from Matt in my tote bag, so I grabbed them to snack on and hold me over until dinner.

"Do you want a strawberry?" I asked Desmond.

"Maybe when I'm done smoking," he answered. "Where'd you get those?"

"From Matt. He got them for my birthday. Student Council was selling them."

"Who's this Matt?"

"I've told you about Matt, remember? He's Andy's old friend. You know, we hang out together at school all the time."

"Well, sounds like your buddy Matt has a crush on you."

"No," I said. "He has a girlfriend."

"He can have a girlfriend and still have a thing for you."

"He seems really happy with his girlfriend."

"Dani, I hate when you act so stupid. He made a point to remember your birthday and bought you chocolates. He wants to fuck you."

"No he doesn't," I said. "Just stop it."

"Maybe he's trying to put you on the back burner for when stuff goes south with his girlfriend, or have you as his side piece."

"That's ridiculous. He doesn't look at me like that, and I don't look at him like that. We've known each other a long time—that's all. And I'm sure not every guy I'm friends with wants to fuck me, just like I don't want to fuck all of them. If that were the case, then we wouldn't be just friends, would we?"

"Dani, you get to an age where innocent friendships with the opposite sex don't exist anymore. You can be cool with coworkers or whatever, sure. But if some guy you don't have to see for work or in class suddenly starts wanting to talk and hang out with you all the time, it's not because he's looking for a pal. There's always an ulterior motive. I know how guys think. You obviously don't."

"Maybe that's just how *you* think! You assume everyone's like you. Maybe I'm the one who should be worried about being cheated on," I snapped.

"Shut the fuck up," Desmond said.

"Whatever. I don't need this," I said. I got up and quickly started putting my outer layers back on. "If this is how you're going to be, I'm going home."

"You're not leaving. We have plans," Desmond said, standing up from his chair.

"You know what, Desmond? I don't care. I don't want to spend my night fighting with you."

"You're such a cunt," he said. "I bet you already sucked his dick."

"You're unbelievable," I told him. I was so utterly disgusted that I had no other words.

I realized I'd left the box of strawberries on the couch, so I went to grab them, my hands trembling in anger as I did, and then Desmond knocked the box right out of them. I watched the strawberries fly out and roll across the carpet. White dog hairs pressed perversely into their moist chocolate coatings.

I blew past Desmond to get my bag and leave from the side door on the stairs. As I reached for the door handle, Desmond clenched me around my arms, squeezing me.

"You're staying here," he said, a low, forceful madness in his voice.

"Let go of me!" I shouted.

Desmond picked me up and pinned me against the wall with his body.

"Get off me!" I said.

He cupped his hand over my mouth, grinding into it with the strength of his wrist.

"You dumb slut, shut your mouth," he whisper-yelled through gritted teeth. "Someone will hear you."

I shook my head around hard to get Desmond's hand away from my mouth. He grabbed my hair at the roots and slammed the back of my head into the wall like a door knocker. Then, he released his hand from my hair with a suddenness, as if spooked by the indelibleness of the act he carried out. His body eased up, allowing me to slip away from him and go swiftly out the door.

As I pulled away in my car, Desmond stood in the front yard without a coat, hands in his pockets, his breath billowing around his parted lips. I felt him watching me until I was out of sight.

EIGHT

Having no particular place to go, I drove around Lakewood for a while, randomly choosing which streets to turn down. I was starving for both food and Desmond. I had so been craving his time and affection before the premature ending of the evening, and quite possibly, I thought, the premature ending of our relationship.

Going home wouldn't make me feel better, and though my grandparents were likely still awake, I couldn't go to their house either. Word would surely get back to my mother that I'd paid them a surprise visit in the middle of the night. She'd grill me about why, even though she'd already know it had something to do with Desmond, and I didn't want to discuss it with her or anyone else. So, I searched for other places or things that might fill the two gnawing holes in the pit of my stomach.

A little Chinese restaurant sufficed for one of them. With only two tiny tables inside for dining, it was mainly a takeout place, which made me feel comfortable to eat there alone. I didn't have the courage to eat by myself in a regular sit-down restaurant where a meal is normally a social experience.

I knew nothing would get rid of my other hunger, but I'd try to dull the pang of it by going to the haunted park to think. I left my car on the street and took my phone and earbuds with me to the black rubber swings. The cold on the swing seat seeped through the bottom of my coat and pants.

The playground sat pretty far away from the road and was slightly uphill. It was a well-lit road, but the light barely reached up the incline. A thought of the lost souls I used to believe hung around there crept into my mind as I looked at the darkness on either side of me. I quickly tried to brush the thought away. I could see the silhouettes of people moving about the big historic homes across the way, and that put me more at ease.

I put in my earbuds and brooded to The Distillers. So are you breaking up with Desmond? I don't want to, but I probably should. He deserves it. He SUCKS! But if I leave to punish him, I'll also be punishing myself, because I don't want to do it. I'll hurt so badly for so long. It's so incredibly unfair that I even have to think about this right now. We aren't supposed to be breaking up. We were supposed to get married someday. And it's my birthday. We already booked everything for Kalahari. I was so excited about it. God DAMNIT. Desmond SUCKS! What a shitty birthday this has been. Fucker! I wonder if I could get away with punching out one of the windows of the school. I'm sure there's no alarm system for those old, empty classrooms. Who would see me up in these shadows?

I bet it wouldn't even hurt right now. I bet it would feel *good*.

My music was replaced with a shrill ring. Desmond was calling. I swiped "reject." I had no desire to talk.

This cycle of incoming call, reject went on for a while until I was enraged by the amount of disruptions he'd caused to "Dismantle Me," which I'd been playing on repeat. I resentfully answered to put an end to the aggravating persistence.

"What, Desmond?" I said.

"Dani …" his voice trailed off. It sounded small and weak. I waited for him to have something more to say.

"Dani," he started again. "I don't know how to even begin to tell you how sorry I am. I know I messed up really bad, and I'm so afraid of losing you. I CANNOT lose you. What we have is too good to throw away over one mistake. I'm begging you, please don't leave."

"Leaving isn't something I want to do, Desmond, but how can I stay when you treat me like that?" I said.

"I promise, it'll never happen again," said Desmond. "I was sorry before it was even over. It was like I was watching myself say and do all these terrible things to you, and I knew it was wrong, but I couldn't stop."

"So let me get this straight. What you're telling me is you lost control of yourself, like you were having an out-of-body experience or something?"

"I realize it probably sounds stupid to you—"

"Yeah, just a little," I interjected.

"OK, well, as much as I hate to admit it, I think a little of my dad's craziness is in me. It beat me this time. And I've been feeling on edge lately because I haven't had any OCs. That'll mess you up. I know that's not a good excuse either, and I need to stop taking them. I'm going to work on it. I swear, if you can find it in your heart to give me another chance, I *will* work on it. This isn't me, Dan."

"God, how much do you use that stuff?" I asked.

"More than I should," he said. "I'm going to calm down on that shit though. Promise."

I sat in silence, the overload of mixed emotions impairing my ability to function and form speech.

"Dan? Are you still there?" said Desmond

It took me another minute to muster, "Yeah. I'm here."

"Please, Dani, you don't have to forgive me right now—I'll earn your forgiveness—but just say you'll give me another chance. Let's go away this weekend like we planned. I want to make your birthday the way it should be. I was so looking forward to it."

"I was too."

"We can still leave on schedule."

He paused and sighed that sigh of being beside yourself that almost sounds like a laugh. Then, he said, "I love you more than life itself, Dani. I was planning to keep you forever you know. Please don't let one thing ruin everything we have and could have."

I said nothing.

"OK, well, that's all I wanted to say, Dani. Hope I'll see you this weekend. Bye."

I liked blaming Desmond's behavior all on sickness and his difficult childhood. He *has* only been violent with me this one time in all our years together, I told myself. The thought of another woman getting all the best parts of him because I couldn't handle his worst parts made me want to die. I viewed myself as a quietly-strong, merciful partner—something no one else had what it took to be. I will fight for him and for us, I decided. I'll save him from the things that plague him and poison our relationship, and we'll make it.

NINE

I was lying with my head at the arm of the couch, propped up by two pillows. Desmond draped a big fleece blanket over me before leaving the room. I sat up and reached for the mug of hot cocoa I'd been letting cool on the coffee table. I tested the temperature by touching the cocoa to my lips. It was just right to drink. I took a couple sips and held the mug, cupped in both my hands, against my cheek to feel its warmth. Chunky snowflakes fell down outside the window.

Desmond returned with a plate of food and set it on the coffee table. He'd breaded and fried chicken breasts and made mashed potatoes, macaroni and cheese, and biscuits as sides.

"Did you find something to watch?" Desmond asked.

"Maybe," I said. "How do you feel about *Friends*?"

He groaned. "I've seen every episode like a million times because of my mom. But I'll watch them again for you if it'll make you happy." He smiled at me teasingly.

I really liked watching *Friends* with my own mom when I was young, but over the years, I forgot how most of the episodes played out. Matt and I had caught some of the show a few days earlier in the Student Center, and since then, I'd had an itch to watch the series all the way through from the beginning.

"Aw, is this your song?" Desmond said, making fun of the way my face lit up when the theme song began. I responded with a glare.

"You're so beautiful, even when you make faces like that," he said. He sat down at the other arm of the couch, put my outstretched legs on top of his lap, and started rubbing my calves and feet. "Every inch of you is perfect to me—from your gorgeous hair, to your lovely curves, to your adorable little toes. I feel like you were made for me. I don't know how I could ever love anyone more."

I leaned forward to kiss the tip of his nose. "I feel the same way about you. I think we were destined to meet."

It's strange how tender, happy moments you have with someone, even when plentiful, can so easily be overshadowed by a few terrible moments with them, and then it's as if all the good stuff never happened at all. Your mind runs a black marker over the life you had with that person, and your entire existence during the period you were together, really, so that remembering any of it requires effort.

"Here, eat, babe," said Desmond, moving the coffee table closer to my reach.

I cut off a piece of chicken and forked it into my mouth. "Aren't you going to eat?" I asked.

"Maybe a little later. My stomach kind of hurts. I'm not that hungry anyway," he said.

This had become the case with Desmond quite often. He either wouldn't eat at all or he'd throw up anything he did. I kept suggesting he go to the doctor, but he refused. It worried me, and, sometimes, even embarrassed me. A few instances that we went out to dinner, he never touched his plate, which caused the servers, and once a manager, to continually ask if there was something wrong with the food. I told him I didn't understand the point in going to a restaurant together if I was going to be the only one eating.

My family also called Desmond out on his eating problem. They had an uncomfortable relationship, so the incident couldn't be easily smoothed over and ended up as another thing to drive a wedge between them.

Grandma Vivian threw my grandpa a birthday party at their house every year. It took a lot of nagging to get Desmond to agree to come, but I just couldn't show up without him this time. My mother had asked me to invite him, and if he wasn't there, I knew she'd make annoying, sarcastic comments about his absence, like, "So will we see Desmond's face again before you're married?" and, "I'm really glad that Desmond could make an appearance today. Oh, wait …"

Desmond became a source of jokes for my parents after Marc and Eric picked him up from our house in Marc's car, which was an old Pontiac Firebird painted black with flames licking up the sides. There was nothing Desmond hated more than to be mocked and unable to shit talk or sucker punch the person doing the mocking, so he would avoid facing my family as much as possible, which only made the jokes increase.

I drove Desmond to the party. The whole extended family was there. My mom and dad were polite and pleasant when Desmond greeted them. My great-grandma Marguerite, Grandma Vivian's mom, who went by Margie, did a good job of compensating for my parents by creating other awkwardness. She'd just had surgery on a cataract. As she was still recovering, brightness was a bother for her, and she worried about dust particles irritating her eye, so she wore her sunglasses inside.

Grandma Margie lived in a storybook-looking home, with pointy gables, moss growing on the roof, and an arched front door sized for hobbits or gnomes, which was fitting, being tiny herself. I definitely got my stature from her side of the family. Her home contained many crocheted quilts and knickknacks, especially angel figurines, and a strong black-licorice smell that I found soothing in spite of not liking the candy; I believe it was from a combination of her Bengay and the homemade anise cookies that her rooster cookie jar was never without. She always had one of those goose statues on the front porch, donning a seasonal outfit and hat.

"Grandma, this is my boyfriend, Desmond," I said to her. I was sure she'd seen him at one of the odd family gatherings he'd actually attended in the last few years, but I didn't think she'd remember. Not because her memory was slipping—she still had the memory of an elephant—but because it was selective.

Grandma Margie turned her head and said, "Oh, it doesn't matter," with a who-cares hand flip and a hopelessness in her voice. "Don't stay with one man. I've been married to three you know."

"Yes, I know this," I said. Though of course she knew that I knew. She just enjoyed hearing herself say it—took pride in it, I think. But it is a novel thing indeed to outlive three spouses.

My dad called her The Black Widow. Her first husband, my real great-grandfather, died in a car accident. Her second husband died of a heart attack, and her third husband from lung cancer.

When I was young and sure of Heaven's existence, I'd wonder how it would play out for Grandma Margie when she got there, what with the three husbands who'd already passed on. Will she be left with the choice of which husband to spend eternity with as they fight over her? Or do we all have personal Heavens where we relive our best memories, like in the show *Supernatural,* allowing each of Grandma Margie's husbands to be with her if they wanted and for her to be with any or all of them?

"She raised all five of her kids on her own while working full-time in a factory," I said to Desmond, giving Grandma Margie a gentle rub on the shoulder. "She's a tough cookie."

"Yeah, life has handed you a lot of lemons, but you always make lemonade, huh, ma?" said Grandma Vivian. She'd come over to hang a coat on the rack behind where Grandma Margie was sitting and to bring her a cup of coffee.

"What?" said Grandma Margie, her face all crinkled up. I could picture the corners of her eyes crinkling too behind her sunglasses. It was an expression my mom inherited. "No. I tell it to go suck them. I make iced tea. Sometimes a rum and coke." She sounded bored when she spoke.

"Dani, will you hand me my purse?" Grandma Margie asked.

"Sure, Grandma," I said. I took her purse off the coat rack and gave it to her. She fumbled around inside it for a minute, muttering some obscenities under her breath, then pulled out a pack of cigarettes and a lighter. She had stopped smoking when she began having children but then started again from the influence of her third husband. She told us it didn't matter what she did to her body anymore because she was at the point in her life when she was basically just waiting to die.

Grandma Margie flicked the lighter a couple times in an attempt to kindle the cigarette.

"Mom!" yelled Grandma Vivian. "You know we don't smoke inside the house. Come on, let's get you outside."

"The sunlight might hurt my eye," said Grandma Margie.

"Oh, Mom, you'll be all right," Grandma Vivian said. "It's warm outside today anyway, like spring. You should enjoy it."

A warm front had come in that weekend, causing temperatures to rise to the mid-40s, which feels tropical when your body has acclimated to the dead of winter in Cleveland.

Grandma Vivian got Grandma Margie up from her chair and helped her put on her coat. She opened the front door and held her hand outside to test the temperature on it. Apparently satisfied with the level of warmth she felt on her skin, she said, "See, Mom, isn't it a nice day?"

"How the hell should I know?" answered Grandma Margie. "I can't see a damn thing."

"You can see just fine. You're almost fully recovered."

"Yes, because you know," said Grandma Margie. "You know how long it takes to feel better after someone has stuck a knife in your eye."

"I could use a cigarette too," said Grandma Vivian, seemingly ignoring her mother's last remark. She took a cigarette from her pack on the gold liquor cabinet and took Grandma Margie by the arm outside with her.

My cousin Jenna arrived, and we sat on the living room couch talking until the food was all done and set out in the kitchen. Jenna was my older cousin by five years and had been like a big sister to me growing up. We had sleepovers all the time, and once she could drive, she'd take me out for girls' nights. We'd go shopping or to dinner, and sometimes to a park or the beach to walk and talk. She introduced me to great vintage resale shops, mom-and-pop restaurants, and bookstores that I'd continue going to on my own later.

When we went to dinner, we always got dessert and coffee afterward. We'd stay there talking all night, getting refill after refill on our coffees, not caring if anyone thought we'd been in the restaurant too long and were hogging all the space from the next people who walked in to dine.

Desmond sat on the couch with us too but was unengaged in our conversation. He had only short answers for the questions Jenna asked him and started fidgeting and playing on his phone.

When Jenna got up to get a second glass of wine, he whispered into my ear, "My stomach hurts."

"I'm sorry," I said. "I can get you some ginger ale."

"I don't want any ginger ale," he said.

"Well I don't know what else to tell you."

There was a spread of spaghetti, meatballs, salad, garlic bread, baked chicken, and roasted red skin potatoes. Desmond still had a full plate after I'd already cleaned mine. He rolled his potatoes around with his fork.

"Do you need me to feed you?" I said jokingly. I cut one of the meatballs on his plate in half and held it up to his mouth. "Do you like airplanes or choo-choos?"

He pushed my fork away from his face.

"Even the smell is making me feel sick now."

"The smell of the meatball is making you sick?" I said, somewhat mockingly. I was tired of his childish refusal to eat and insistence on being mopey. I hadn't realized how loudly I was talking. I'd had some wine myself, and sometimes alcohol causes me to project my voice.

Then, practically the whole room was staring at Desmond.

"You don't like the meatballs?" said Grandma Vivian, looking taken aback and concerned.

No one in the history of the world since Grandma Vivian had been in it hadn't liked her meatballs. They were a staple of every Carmino family gathering and a huge hit anywhere else they were tasted. Some of the Morans had enjoyed them so much at the birthday parties and cookouts my parents had hosted for both sides of our family that they requested them for their events, like my cousin Julie's graduation party and my grandpa's seventieth birthday. They were nothing like the tough, flavorless meatballs I'd been served at many casual restaurants. Grandma Vivian's meatballs held their shape on a plate, but once in your mouth, their moist, cheesy centers would just melt, like the best kind of cake. She made them using some combination of a recipe handed down through her mom's family and the one from Grandpa Adrian's parents—a compromise, she called it.

Nobody else knew Grandma Vivian's meatball-making technique. It troubled me to think that if Grandma Vivian was no longer with us, her meatballs wouldn't be either—not just because I would never get to eat them again, of course, but because I wanted the tradition of them to live on so that a part of her would too.

Bernadette and I used to help make them sometimes when we were young. It was a long process. Grandma Vivian would say, "If you're not going to make at least 100, there's no point in making them at all." So, it would be a whole night for us, with pizza or Chinese takeout and movies from Grandpa Adrian's favorite movie rental store.

Every time I slept over as a kid, my grandpa would take me and whoever was also over that evening—my brothers or cousins or Bernadette—to this little corner video store, which was still a common thing at the time, to pick out movies. When we got home, if there were a lot of kids, he'd tear a piece of paper into small slips and write numbers on them—one for each of us. We'd draw the slips from a bowl, and the number you drew was the number your movie would be in the watchlist order.

Anyway, Grandma Vivian was right about the meatballs. She'd make about 150 for family gatherings, and they'd all get eaten somehow, or at the very least, the few remaining when everyone was heading out were competitively snagged for taking home.

Bernadette and I dubbed making meatballs with my grandma "meatballing." Grandma Vivian would put on 1950s and '60s pop and rock in the dining room to listen to while we cooked. Bern and I later made a playlist of all our favorite songs she'd play that we called "Meatballing Music."

When we were meatballing, I never paid attention to exactly how much of what went into the meat. Bern and I just had fun chopping stuff and mixing everything together until the meat was the right color and texture, at which point my grandma would encourage us to taste a tiny bit of it as a final test of flavor perfection before it was all rolled and too late to add anything it lacked.

"Don't listen to your grandma. You don't want to eat raw beef and eggs," Grandpa Adrian would say. He periodically popped into the kitchen to see how things were coming along and to give help where needed.

"It's fine. You can spit it out after you judge the flavor. I do it all the time. That's how you really know you made it right. Try it," Grandma Vivian would insist.

And my grandpa would go, "Nah nah nah nah," shaking his head, and she'd be all, "Come on, it's fine," and then there'd be more, "Nah nah nah nah," and eventually, my grandma would throw her hands up in surrender and say, "OK, I guess no one else has to taste it but me," and we'd just take her word for it that it was good.

I decided one year in college that I wanted to learn the meatball and sauce recipes, so I went to my grandparents' house before Easter to help cook. I asked Grandma Vivian to tell me all of what she was putting in the meat and her sauce and how much and how long everything was cooked and at what temperatures, and I wrote it down so I wouldn't forget. She never measured anything out when she cooked. She said she just judged it.

The first time I attempted the sauce and meatballs on my own, I painstakingly followed my instructions, but the flavor of the meatballs was all wrong, and the second time, it was all wrong again.

So amid everyone's perplexity over how Desmond could not like Grandma Vivian's meatballs, I quickly tried to recover for him.

"It's not the meatballs," I said. "It's him. He hasn't been feeling well. His stomach is too upset to eat anything."

The cake was brought out soon afterward. As the candles were being lit, Aunt Linda, who's married to my mom's brother, Marty, said to Desmond, "So does the smell of the cake make you sick too?"

"Yeah, are you going to throw up on it?" Dylan, my cousin Jack's kid, chimed in.

"I'm fine," Desmond said.

As cake slices and ice cream and whiskey shots were being handed around, Desmond pulled me aside in the kitchen.

"Hey, can we get going?" he asked. "I'm ready."

"Well, I'm not. I want to enjoy my family more, and no one else is leaving yet."

He sighed at the ceiling.

"Do you mind if I leave then?"

"Fine," I said.

Eric came to the house for him.

After he left, I was back on the couch with Jenna, another glass of wine in my hand, and she said to me quietly, 'Hey, um … is Desmond on drugs?"

"I don't know," I told her. I was surprised she'd asked, and I honestly *didn't* know whether he still was or wasn't.

"I think he might be," she said with one of those pursed-lip half smiles people make when they're trying to give you bad news as nicely as possible.

TEN

It was the middle of the night, and Desmond and I were driving through the Cleveland Metroparks. This was a favorite pastime of ours. I loved the way the bare, white branches of the Sycamores glowed mystically against the black sky like the face of a barn owl, and Desmond loved long drives.

We listened to bands we agreed on. Starting with Alice In Chains, we went to Stone Temple Pilots to Metallica to Pantera. Then, we played a medley of pop-punk from the early 2000s—basically the sound of our childhoods—featuring Sum 41, Blink-182, The All-American Rejects, Simple Plan, and Green Day. Desmond sang along loudly to every song with his left arm hanging out of the window, as usual. I sang quietly and reminded him for the umpteenth time that he shouldn't drive with his arm out the window in case some calamity were to occur in which it could get chopped off.

I hated to ruin the peace we were enjoying by asking the question, but I couldn't get it off my mind, so I did.

"Desmond, I've been wondering something." It was harder to just come out with it than I thought it would be.

"Yeah?" he said.

"Are you still taking pills?"

He paused for a moment, then cleared his throat.

"Yes. I am."

"OK. At least you're honest about it I guess, but why? Why do you do it?"

"I do it because it makes me feel better, if I'm being straight up."

"It makes you feel better how?"

"In all ways. Physically, mentally. It calms my stomach and my stress."

"But isn't it probably the reason your stomach hurts in the first place? Like from dependency and withdrawal?"

"I'm not dependent. Trust me. I could stop completely if I wanted. I choose not to, because, like I said, it makes me feel better. I've toned it down a lot though."

"I still don't understand it. There are other solutions for mental distress. Maybe we can get you a therapist."

"Of course you don't understand," he said.

"What's that supposed to mean?"

"Dani, when you live every day with the kind of darkness I do, you need something to dull the pain. I grew up dirt poor with a maniac for a father and had to watch my mother, the only person who ever really loved me as a kid, suffer through countless surgeries, and now I have to see her sit in pain every day of her life. I wake up sometimes thinking I can't survive one more day in my own head. No kind of meditation or Zen bullshit can work on someone as fucked as me, and shrinks are bullshit too. They charge $100 an hour to judge you and tell you things you could figure out yourself. They don't care about you—they just want you to keep coming back so they can take your money. The world offers no comfort, Dani. Sometimes the best thing you can do is take something that helps you forget it."

"I don't offer any comfort to you?" I said.

"It's not that. You just can't relate to me, so you can only help so much. You live in a gingerbread world. Your family put on this show of perfection your whole life and told you that God will take care of you. It's like believing that Santa is watching you. They shielded you from reality. You don't know real problems. Your biggest problem is that you can't decide between the opportunities in front of you—some of which I could never dream of."

"I don't know real problems?" I laughed in disbelief. "And you have more opportunities than you think. You just don't want to put in the effort it requires to see them through. Like, you would've gotten more aid to pay for college than me because of your parents' financial situation. You chose not to do the things you have to do to go to college. Nothing was stopping you but you."

"Whatever, man," said Desmond, shaking his head. "Like it would've been just that easy. You know what? I take back what I said. What's really your biggest problem is that you set your expectations too high. It's because you think too much of yourself, and you're used to having everything. You really believe your future will turn out the way you see it in your dreams, just because you feel you deserve it. One day, you're going to find out that you can't have the whole fucking world, and you'll be sorely disappointed. Maybe it'll bring you down closer to my level."

I didn't speak again for what felt like hours, until Desmond finally asked if I was ready to go home. I told him yes. I could have counted on one hand how many times I blinked as I kept my eyes fixed on the passing forests.

It surprised me to hear Desmond paint my life as one of such entitlement and abundance, as if I were born with a silver spoon in my mouth. Kids like that had dads who went to work in white-collared shirts and ties and rented beach houses for their families' vacations every year and gave their kids allowances. My dad went to work in a hard hat and steel toe boots. He was a carpenter. He'd almost been a professional boxer. He said he left fighting to go into construction because my mom wouldn't marry him if he didn't do something else—that the fighting life made her too concerned about his health. She told us that wasn't true, although she never gave a real explanation as to what she told him—just, "Oh, I never said that."

My dad helped out at a local boxing and MMA gym as a trainer when we were growing up to stay around it. He would take my brothers and me sometimes to watch and let us hit the bag or hold mitts for us. He taught us fundamentals too. He'd say to me, "Such a sweet girl, but you've got that Moran mean streak."

My mom worked as a secretary for the Catholic Diocese of Cleveland, which could pay her only a meager salary. My parents never once took us on a family vacation or gave us allowances, because they couldn't afford to.

I mostly used the money I made under the table from Carmin's to go out on the weekends with before I was legally old enough to hold a job, and I occasionally had babysitting money. To be more economical, Bern and I would shop at thrift stores or buy outfits that we both liked on ourselves and could trade off. My brothers and I only got new clothes for our birthdays or Christmas. The nice thing about Catholic school was not needing a lot of clothes, because you wore a uniform every day.

And OK, yeah, we went to Catholic school, but Holy Rosary was far from fancy. The infrastructure and learning materials were old and dingy, and the extracurriculars and opportunities for academic enrichment were limited. Catholic school, to us, and to the majority of the kids there, was simply the alternative to the abysmal city schools before charter schools became more common. Nearly 100 percent of our tuition was waived anyway because of my mom's job. The diocese made her a deal where we could attend at almost no cost in exchange for her health insurance. She didn't really need it since my dad was able to insure all of us through his union's family health plan.

The early 2000s were particularly difficult for my parents financially. There was a period when work was scarce for my dad. In those days, my parents struggled to scrounge enough money to fill their gas tanks and buy food.

I remember my mom sending my dad and me to the store one evening when our fridge and cupboards had become bare with a $20 bill as our budget. My mom instructed my dad, tears welling up in her eyes, just to get food for our school lunches for the week. That was most important. She had to ask sister, Jackie, or my grandparents for grocery money sometimes, which I knew she didn't like to do. I once overheard her telling my dad as much in their bedroom after she'd gotten off the phone with Aunt Jackie. The door had been cracked open. She said, "I've never been needy. I hate feeling like this. It's not me."

Someday though, my mom would get a job as an admissions director in a hospital where she'd make much more money, and work would pick up permanently for my father as revitalization of the city ramped up. He'd become a supervisor too, earning him a raise. After my brothers and I were moved out, they'd buy their dream home. Their fridge and cupboards would always be stocked when I came to visit. They'd drive the cars they wanted and never not have enough money for gas, and they'd vacation every year.

When I got to college, I was amazed to learn that so many of my new acquaintances had grown up in houses with these extra rooms they called dens and rec rooms and studies, and that some had their own private bathrooms. I thought of the one full bathroom in my family's house and how it was getting ready for school in it when we were young: I'd be doing my hair in the mirror above the sink while Andy was using it to meticulously scrub his face and apply a thick layer of acne lotion. He never got zits but was paranoid he'd wake up covered in them if he didn't take said measures, and then he'd freak that his skin was drying out from them. I'd accidentally elbow him as I combed up at my roots for volume or when I raised my arms to tie my hair into a ponytail. He'd get all pissed and go, "Dani, watch what you're doing!" and "God, Dani!"

Mikey would be cutting in between Andy and me to brush his teeth. He'd wet his toothbrush and squeeze more toothpaste onto it after each time he spat, so the process could've gone on all day if it wasn't for Andy always saying, "That's it! You're done!" taking away his toothbrush and putting it back in the toothbrush holder our whole family used.

Patrick would get up last. Never minding the other three of us in the bathroom, he'd walk over to the toilet, drop his pants, and take his first-thing-in-the-morning pee. We'd avert our eyes. Then, Patrick would take my place at the sink, and I'd stand behind him, helping Mikey comb his hair. We were a cluster of bumping bodies in the small space.

The memories of my upbringing didn't feel like they fit Desmond's perspective of it, but I figured it was relative to his own upbringing. I wondered if the people who I thought grew up with more extravagance viewed their circumstances as the norm, which is how I'd viewed my own.

Most of my school acquaintances outside my fields of study were made through Gabby's new boyfriend, Cameron Brenton. Cameron bounced around from major to major. He started in Engineering, moved to Political Science—we'd actually had a class together—went next to Business, and switched once more to Acting. I knew from being in class with him that he was one for dramatics, so Acting suited him I guess. He carried himself regally, often remarking that his parents were both doctors who met in Harvard Medical School, which seemed to boost his self-regard of princeliness.

Cameron was never without his sidekick—this guy who refused to wear closed-toe shoes. It was flip flops or some other type of sandal all the time, even in the winter. I supposed he could have gotten by taking the innerlink through campus when it was cold. The innerlink is a glass-enclosed walkway that connects the main parking garages and the majority of buildings on campus to shield people from the harsh elements. What was more peculiar about this guy though was that his feet were always sooty, like he'd gone running barefoot along a muddy river bank and hadn't washed after.

Cameron told Gabby and me that he might know a girl who'd be interested in being our bassist—the girlfriend of one of his drama friends. That girl was Layla. The School of Theater and Dance was hosting their annual fundraiser in the auditorium of the Liberal Arts College, and Cameron told me I should come with Gabby because Layla would be there with her boyfriend, and it would give the three of us a chance to meet. Oh, and also because he wanted me to support the fundraiser.

"Please, Dani. Please come support us poor drama kids," he said to me on his knees in one of the study areas of the Student Center when he came to find Gabby. He was always over the top like that.

He had to go to the event early to help set up, so I went with Gabby. Once we found Cameron, he took Gabby around by the arm, showing her off to all his instructors and classmates she hadn't met.

I moseyed around the silent auction tables alone. I couldn't afford to bid on anything, but I did buy the $40 ticket, so I still contributed in some way, I told myself.

When I felt done looking at the auction, I wandered over to my assigned table in the dining area. It was a large round table with eight seats. Four of them were for me, Gabby, Cameron, and his sidekick. The other four were for people I didn't know. A couple of them were already occupied by girls having a quiet conversation that seemed rather personal, as they were turned tightly toward each other like they were trying to shelter the words they were speaking. They paused briefly to smile at me and then went back to whatever they were talking about.

A moment later, a guy and another girl came over. The girl sat next to me, the guy on her other side.

"Hi! I'm Katrin," she said.

"I'm Dani."

"Are you in the Theater or Dance program?"

"No, I'm studying Journalism and Political Science."

"Oh wow, good for you."

"Thanks. What about you?"

"I'm majoring in Dance with a minor in English."

"Impressive," I said. She looked like a ballerina, with half of her shiny hair wrapped into a perfect bun high on her head, which highlighted her prominent cheek bones and long, slender neck, and the rest of her hair hanging sleekly down her back.

"This is my boyfriend, Jordan," said Katrin, pulling on the sleeve of the guy with her. "He's studying Business." He said hello to me and reached across the table to shake my hand.

They asked who I was there for, and I explained my connection to Cameron. Then, Cameron's sidekick showed up and took the empty seat beside me. I attempted to stealthily inspect his footwear. I always felt compelled to see if he'd changed it up. He had not.

When I was done checking him out, I discovered Katrin staring at me inquisitively.

"Are you Greek?" she asked.

"No."

"Jewish?"

"No, not Jewish either." I laughed at the randomness of the questions. I'd been getting a lot of inquiries about my ethnicity since starting college.

"Oh. My family vacationed in Greece last summer, and you remind me of the local girls. Just something about your look ... I don't know ... I sound stupid." She looked down into her lap and laughed.

"Did you say you vacationed in Greece?" asked one of the other girls at the table.

"Yes," said Katrin.

"Have you been to Thessaloniki? I studied abroad there last year."

"Yes, as a matter of fact! We did a major cities tour. The food and nightlife in Thessaloniki are really great. Have you studied abroad anywhere else?" Katrin asked.

"Just Germany," the girl said.

"Germany is amazing," said Katrin.

"I'd really like to study abroad again this summer in the Netherlands, but I'm not sure how I'll pay for it."

"I went to Amsterdam with some friends the summer after I graduated high school," Jordan butted in. "You should *totally* study there. You'll have the time of your life."

"I'd also love to get to Japan or South Korea before the end of college," the girl said.

"Mmm. Mhmm," said Jordan, nodding in approval.

"That's probably wishful thinking though," the girl continued. "My parents already give me a monthly living stipend, plus they pay for my tuition and dorm and stuff, so I don't think they'd give me any more money for school trips. I don't think I could save enough of my stipend money by the time I'd owe for the Netherlands trip either, and, I mean, who really has time for a job with class full-time and studying?"

"Yeah, exactly," Katrin said.

"You're only in college once though," said Jordan. "They might understand."

"I told you, write a persuasive essay!" said the girl's friend. "When I was assigned to write one for my high school English class, I did it about why my dad should cover a trip to Brazil with my art club, and it convinced him."

"No," the other girl said hopelessly. "I don't think an essay will convince my parents."

"A personal loan!" Jordan said. "My parents take out a personal loan for me every year for my living expenses while I'm at school. You could definitely use one to pay for Greece."

"My parents just send me to school with one of their credit cards for my living expenses," Persuasive Essay Girl said with a smug grin.

It made me a little nauseous the way they were all so comfortable living off their parents—so entitled to their money. They continued talking about their excursions abroad like they were trying to one up each other. I wanted to shrink away from the table.

I turned to Cameron's sidekick.

"The only other country I've been to is Canada, and I happen to hold a job *while* going to school," I whispered to him.

"What do you know? Same here!" We giggled at our little inside joke.

"I'm Dani, by the way," I said to him. "I don't think we've ever formally met."

"No, I guess we haven't," he said. "I'm Nick."

"So where do you work, Nick?" I wondered if his job was the reason for his perpetually dirty feet. He could be a landscaper, or helping at a local farm, or a ... chimney sweep perhaps?

"I work at a car wash called Al's Auto Wash."

Go figure—he works with soap and water all day.

I was relieved when Gabby and Cameron finally came over to tell me Layla was there. I left the event right after our conversation with Layla concluded, because I was not going back to my table.

ELEVEN

We played a show one night in Kent. It was with our second bassist, Valerie. We had a high turnaround for bassists.

Valerie's primary instrument was actually piano. She also knew guitar and dabbled in ukulele. With her musical experience, she was able to pull off bass well enough to work for our group.

Cameron recorded our set on his phone and sent it to all of us. I liked having recordings of our sets mainly for critiquing and constructive reasons, but that night, I was eager to hear it purely for relishing. I thought we'd sounded really tight. I was still buzzing and glowing after we packed up our cars to go home.

Desmond came to the show with me. When we got back to the highway, I asked him if he'd mind listening to the set in the car. He said he didn't.

I connected my phone to the stereo and found the file from Cameron. I couldn't get it to open for some reason. I kept messing around with it while being careful not to take my eyes off the road for more than a moment, but it turned out that a moment was still too long. I was completely caught off guard when someone pulled out in front of us from the median. Being in a rural-ish area, our surroundings were dark, and there were no high-mast lights, so visibility wasn't great.

I didn't think I could slow down in time to prevent rear-ending the other car, so I steered up onto the grass off the side of the road. My car clunked and jerked as I tried to decelerate on the pit-and-rock-riddled stretch of land.

"What the fuck?!" Desmond yelled.

I swerved right to avoid what looked like a steep drop-off ahead, turning the car 180 degrees from the highway, and then was finally able to stop. "I'm sorry! I thought I was going to hit the other person," I said.

"Jesus Christ," said Desmond, his hands over his eyes.

I was trembling and sweating.

"You could have fucking killed us, Dani," Desmond said. "You're too worried about your shitty band to be smart. You should have asked me to fuck with your phone so you could drive."

"If you think my band is shitty, why did you even come?" I said.

"Because you're my girlfriend," he answered.

"You don't have to be here just because I'm your girlfriend. Don't come next time, OK?"

"Oh, don't even start with your bullshit, Dani. I'm not in the mood."

"I'm being completely serious," I said. "If you really don't want to come, then don't."

"Fine. Whatever," said Desmond. He turned toward his window, and I heard him mutter "stupid bitch" under his breath.

"What did you just call me?" I said.

"I didn't say anything."

"Yes, you did. I heard you."

"Then why did you ask?"

A lump suddenly emerged in my throat, and tears welled up in my eyes.

"God, you're too sensitive," Desmond said. "I have to tiptoe around you and talk to you like a little kid, because if I'm too real with you, or I cuss at you because I'm mad, or I say something that offends you in any way, you can't handle it! I'm so sick of it."

My tears began plopping onto the steering wheel.

"Are you kidding me? You're going to cry now? I can't deal with this shit. No other guy would either. Not for you. You're no prize." This only made we cry harder. Desmond put his hands over his eyes again and rubbed his forehead in frustration.

"So are we ever going to get out of here?" he asked, his voice raised. "Can we go the fuck home now? You've wasted enough of my night."

I ignored him and tried to focus on controlling my breathing. I wiped the wetness from my face and steering wheel.

"Hey, I'm fucking talking to you!" Desmond yelled.

I turned to tell him that his shouting wasn't helping anything. When I did, I was backhanded over my mouth and nose. I felt my teeth cut into the inner part of my bottom lip, and blood began dribbling down my chin from my nostril. I pinched my nose with one hand, grabbed my keys in the other, and got out of the car. I didn't know what I was going to do next, but I knew I wanted to be away from Desmond. I started aimlessly walking down the road as fast as my shins could handle.

Desmond caught up with me. "Dani, where are you going?" he said.

"Away from you!" Little flecks of blood sprayed from my lips at him as I shouted, and I could feel the bottom one swelling. I turned to keep walking, but Desmond wrapped his arms around me to stop me.

"Dani, I swear I didn't mean to do that. You weren't answering me, so I tried to wave my hand in front of you to get your attention, and you turned into me. It was an accident. I wasn't trying to hit you."

"Well you did! It was hard," I said to him.

"It probably wasn't as hard as you think. You got freaked out because you started bleeding, and you're upset. We both know your nose bleeds easily."

He was right. It did. I'd had problems my whole life with nosebleeds. It would bleed when the air was too dry, too cold, too hot, and often in school classrooms. If I'd been having a spell of frequent nosebleeds, twitching my nose to get an itch or sleeping with my face pressed into my pillow could trigger one.

"Come on, Dani. Give me your keys and I'll drive home. Where are you going to go anyway?"

I gave Desmond my keys, and we got back into the car to head home. My neck and arms were streaked with blood by this point. I took off my shirt and held it tightly to my nostril while I pinched the bridge of my nose so I could get the blood to clot. My nosebleeds went on forever sometimes.

After we pulled into Desmond's driveway, he said to me, "Dani, you look terrible. You can't go home like that. Stay here while I get you something to cover up with."

He went into the house through the basement door and came back out with a fresh t-shirt for me to put on.

"Why don't you just come inside and let me help you clean yourself up. You still look awful with blood all over your skin like that," Desmond said to me outside the open door of the passenger side, from which I still hadn't moved. Pumping so much adrenaline over the course of the evening, from getting on stage to the incidents that occurred when we left the venue, had left my body a dead motor.

I was too ashamed to go home in the state I was in, so I let Desmond help me peel myself off the car seat, and we went to the basement. He gave me a warm, soapy washcloth but then followed me into the bathroom and insisted on doing all the work wiping me down, taking care to be thorough and delicate. Afterward, he drenched my dirty shirt and bra in stain remover spray and put them into the washing machine.

"I'm not sure these stains will come out, but worth a shot," he said.

I was surprised and slightly disturbed by how nice he was suddenly being.

"Do you need anything?" he asked. "How 'bout a drink?"

"Sure," I said. "Some water would be good."

He went upstairs to get the water. I sat on the couch. Lee was asleep by the stairs. I looked at him and thought, we can relate to one another.

I slowly sipped the water Desmond brought me until I wasn't thirsty anymore, and then, still feeling lifeless, I rested my head on the arm of the couch and closed my eyes. I ended up sleeping through the night. I woke with a blanket draped over me. Desmond was asleep in his bed.

I found my bra and shirt inside the dryer. Both were covered in brown spots. I put the bra on because no one would see the spots anyway, and outside the house, I felt naked not wearing a bra. I tossed the shirt into the trash. Sadly, it had been a favorite—my Sleater-Kinney shirt. I bought it at their show. Gabby went with me. It was one of the best times we ever had together.

I took an old sweatshirt of Desmond's that he let me borrow all the time and didn't think he'd miss. He said it had gotten too small for him.

"Desmond," I whispered into his ear as I lightly shook his shoulder. "I'm going home. I have some things I need to do."

"OK, babe," he said groggily. "Call me later." He smooched the air, hinting to give him a kiss. I kissed him goodbye.

I didn't go home right away. Instead, I went to a nearby city called Berea. One of my favorite places to go as a child was Wallace Lake in Berea. My mom used to take us there, and her parents took her there. It has a beach and a walking trail and is part of the Cleveland Metroparks.

I've always remembered this one time in particular that I walked the trail with my mom. I hadn't started school in the big elementary building at Holy Rosary yet—they have a separate building for kindergarten—so I couldn't have been older than six. We were holding hands, and my mom said to me, "I hope we never fight when you get older like some mothers and daughters do. I hope we stay like this."

In Berea's shopping district is a park-like island of land with a clock tower in the middle of it called the Berea Triangle, which is basically the town square, but, as the name would indicate, triangular. The facades of the mom-and-pop shops surrounding it are all old-world style. North of the shopping district, historic buildings house a small, private university, which adds a pinch of that college-town vibe to the area, and there are streets of big, beautiful Victorian houses.

I went inside a café a block away from the Triangle. I ordered a cappuccino and a piece of cake. Normally, I wouldn't eat cake at just any old time, but I realized I was starving, and my emotional state was such that I felt like I'd fallen to the bottom of an elevator shaft, so I was going to have whatever I wanted for breakfast without a care.

I sat at the bar along the window. I turned slightly to watch the people sitting behind me. There were two old men merrily chit-chatting with each other in some arm chairs by the front door. At one table, a middle-aged, scholarly-looking man was deep in a book. At another table, two teenage boys were trading cards. There was also an adult couple quietly talking and sipping coffee as they stared outside dreamily, two twenty-something-year-old women smiling almost incessantly as they conversed and laughing softly, as if they were just taking turns telling light-hearted jokes to each other and every single one was landing, and a priest or other type of clergy member playing checkers with a friend.

Everyone seemed so at peace with themselves and the world—so charmed. I saw myself as a freight train wrecking into their pleasant little place. I was waiting for them all to start noticing their equilibriums being offset by me, the pariah.

I didn't want to feel like a pariah, or like someone's mistreated dog. I also didn't want to let go of Desmond. I knew things wouldn't always be as I wished they were, no matter how hard I tried to make them so. By the time I finished my cappuccino and cake, I decided that out of the things I didn't want, I'd have to choose breaking up.

TWELVE

"You know what you need?" Gabby said to me on a day when I was particularly mopey. We were lounging on some couches in the Student Center before our late-afternoon classes.

"What?"

"You need to go out with someone new."

"You mean I need a rebound?"

"Well, you don't have to think of it that way," said Gabby. "The next person you date could end up working out long-term. I think I might actually know someone you'd like."

"Oh yeah? Who?"

"One of Cameron's friends."

"Not the guy with the dirty feet ..." I said.

"Who?" Gabby asked.

"Nick. I think that's his name."

"No, not Nick. Liam McDaniel. He's really handsome and smart and sweet. And single."

"All right. I could be open to this," I said.

Liam *was* really handsome and smart and sweet. His sandy-blond hair fell around his shirt collar. His eyes were olive green, and he usually wore black, thick-rimmed glasses, which I thought framed his eyes in such a way that made their color appear even more brilliant, unlike when I wore glasses. I thought my glasses just made my eyes look smaller and dull. His major was Biology, and he had plans of going to medical school.

Liam had been a close high school friend of Cameron. They met in the school's a capella group.

"A capella? Really? I would never have guessed you were into that," I told Liam after he mentioned it to me. We were at dinner in the Cleveland Flats, a restaurant and retail area on the banks of the Cuyahoga River. Trying new restaurants was sort of our thing. Liam was a foodie, and I always enjoyed a dinner date, especially if it was one I could get dolled up for, which was the case with most of the places we went. Liam was a sharp dresser and never at a loss for a classy dinner-date outfit himself. He would speak of each thing he tried on his plate like he was orating a review, with me as his scribe. We kept a shared mental list of our top-favorite dishes.

"Yes. I'm quite a good singer, if I do say so myself," said Liam.

"I bet you are."

"You don't believe me."

"No, I really do," I said.

Then, all of a sudden, he broke out in song right there in our booth. He sang "Baby I Need Your Loving" by the Four Tops. I almost fell onto the floor laughing.

"I'm so … sorry," I barely got out between gasps for air, as I was still cracking up. "You're great. I just … wasn't expecting you to start singing right here."

"Sure. Sure," he said, looking bitter. I didn't know if he was actually upset or playing. "I'm sorry I'm not a cool punk rock singer like you."

"I'm being completely and whole-heartedly sincere," I said, having finally gotten a hold of myself. I reached across the table and took his hand in mine. "You do have a beautiful voice, and I actually love that song."

"Me too." He smiled.

Liam appreciated the same old music I did— '50s and '60s pop and rock, Big Band, Swing. We had a common interest in many other genres as well, like '90s alternative rock, modern alternative rock, new wave, post-punk, shoegaze, and trip-hop. We'd put on Portishead or My Bloody Valentine and lose the whole night in conversation on his bed. We'd talk about politics, religion, social issues, books, our families, random areas of study that piqued our interest, career plans, and hopes for our futures. He had a compulsion to tell me facts about outer space and rare animal species. When he went down a rabbit hole with theories on alien life forms, I'd teasingly tell him he was getting too nerdy on me.

I enjoyed trying to intrigue him with my philosophical ponderings. If I posed a rhetorical question, he'd answer with these proverbial statements, which annoyed me at first but grew to be endearing— like, when I said, "I wonder why I experience life as Dani Moran. Why was I not born into some other mind and body, some other family?" he said, "Rather than ask why you are not someone else, ask why you are lucky to be you." I laughed and told him he sounded like a fortune cookie.

I liked Liam. I liked all his good qualities. But I loved Desmond. I wanted so badly to love Liam instead. I beat myself up over it. I despised myself for it.

The distraction of a new relationship and the rush of what seemed could be a new chapter in my life helped me push my love for Desmond down deep enough that I convinced myself it wasn't there anymore for a little while. Once all the stirrings of beginnings inside me settled, my longing for Desmond re-emerged. At first, it was intermittent—mostly at times my mind wandered. Then, it became a constant. When I was with other people, he was always in the back of my mind. When I was alone, he was the focus of my thoughts. I couldn't push my feelings back down again no matter how hard I tried.

We wrote love letters and poems back and forth in high school. No other boy had ever written me anything. I kept his letters and poems in a band-sticker-decorated shoebox under my bed that held other sentimental things I'd saved over the years—cards from my grandparents, funny notes from friends, Ardis Alchemy concert flyers, favorite old photos. Desmond kept my letters and poems in a metal My Chemical Romance lunchbox from middle school on the shelf by his computer.

I started opening that shoebox every night, poring over his words.

One of his letters read, "My every thought, my every breath, ends on you."

Mine too.

I desperately wanted to know what Desmond was up to and didn't want to know at the same time. Seeing that he'd moved on, even though I had, would kill me.

I broke down one day and started checking his social media pages. I was relieved to find only new photos of him playing music—no photos with other girls or mentions of them.

I kept things low-key online myself regarding my dating life. I didn't want Desmond to find out there was someone else, in case he was also checking.

After a couple weeks of torturing myself with frequent views of Desmond's social media, I decided to de-activate all of mine. I figured that way, I'd stop feeling inclined to creep and wondering all the time if he was doing it too. In spite of this, it became increasingly difficult to eat, sleep, pay attention in class, be the girlfriend I should have been to Liam, and be happy or excited about anything. I had that gnawing hunger like a hole in the pit of my stomach again, an unfed addiction. I was no longer fully functioning but still functioning enough not to die. I started to wish I would die. Some nights, I prayed for my heart to stop in my sleep and put me out of my misery. But alas, I continued to wake every morning, feeling the same.

I began to question whether I *had* overreacted about the whole nosebleed incident in my car. Maybe it was all like Desmond said it was—a misunderstanding, an accident—and I had twisted the reality of it. And I thought back on the time he grabbed me by my hair ... Was it as big of a deal as I'd made it? He didn't *hit* me. And all the things he said that hurt me ... Had he truly meant them? Do words really matter? Music and TV are full of ugly language, and no one bats an eye. At parties, huddles of girls fervently sing along with songs that say things like "dumb little ho" and "suck my dick, bitch," their red Solo cups raised in the air. So maybe I'm the only one who minds words like that. Maybe I am too sensitive, and I gave up on Desmond and me too soon. Could everything that happened be forgiven?

The fiend in my head began whispering to me new ways to keep tabs on Desmond. It didn't need social media. I tried not to listen to it, but still, I'd find myself taking little detours past Desmond's house on my way home from school or band practice. I was disappointed when I didn't catch a glimpse of him. I imagined spotting him on his way to the corner store, pulling over on the side of the road, and running to him. I would lie to myself that it was totally by chance we'd crossed paths. I'd ask him to take me back. But another part of me thought I really shouldn't do those things, so it was also a relief not to see him.

I had a Friday afternoon class that semester. After it one day, Valerie and I got dinner and hung out at a bar and grill in the Student Center. It was well into the evening when I left for home.

I wasn't able to find parking that morning in the garage I normally parked in because of some paid event taking place, so I had to park in one of the far garages that's not connected to the innerlink. The shortest, quickest route there required me to pass Flanders'. People were lined up against the brick of

Flanders' building, waiting to get into whatever show was going on.

With the immense heaviness in my heart, I thought the weight of someone's gaze resting on me could be the tipping point that took me to the ground, so I crossed the street to the sidewalk farthest from the crowd. I walked fast with my head down.

I felt a tug on my sleeve from behind me. I whirled around defensively, and there was Desmond.

"Dani," he said, looking deeply into my eyes with a sad, disbelieving half-smile.

Now that we actually *were* crossing paths totally by chance, I was so stunned that I thought I might faint. My vision wavering from the lightheadedness, I clutched the side of my head.

"Dani, are you OK?" Desmond asked, placing his hands on my shoulders as if to help keep me from losing my balance.

"I'm fine," I answered, pulling away.

Desmond was still staring right into my face. "Wow. My memory of your beauty doesn't even do it justice," he said.

"You're here for a show I take it?" I said, ignoring his last remark.

"Yeah. Just watching."

"Well, have a nice time," I told him, and I turned to be on my way.

"Hey," Desmond said, pulling on my sleeve again. "You're going to go just like that? Can I talk to you for a minute?"

"I really can't," I said to him.

Before I could process what he was going to attempt and stop him, Desmond's lips were on mine. I didn't kiss him back.

"I'm dating someone else," I blurted out once I'd managed to brush him away.

"Oh." He blinked hard a couple times, looked down, and went silent for a moment. Then, he drew a breath in heavily, like he was struggling to breathe at all. "Well, that … kind of breaks my heart. I honestly haven't been able to think about looking for someone else yet." To hear that made me feel guilty and cheap.

"Do you love him?" Desmond asked.

"I don't know," I replied, unable to look him in the eye.

"Do you still love me?"

I answered with only a sigh as I stared at my foot kicking around on the ground.

"I know our relationship wasn't perfect," said Desmond. "No relationships are. Most of our problems were probably my fault. I should have been better. I kick myself every day for not being better to you, Dani. But regardless of what someone has to offer, if you don't have love, none of the other things matter."

Sadly, I knew he was right. Despite all the things Liam had going for himself and how sweet he was to me, my pining wouldn't stop. To love the idea of someone is not necessarily to love them.

Desmond took my hand and clasped it between his. I wanted to kiss him this time. We kissed passionately.

"Can I meet you later tonight?" he asked.

"I don't think so. Not tonight," I said. I was supposed to be spending the night with Liam. I wanted him to know what was going on and put an end to things between us before starting anything with Desmond again. "I need to take care of something first."

"I'm never going to let you get away from me again," Desmond said to me, touching my cheek.

When I went to Liam's dorm later, I told him about running into Desmond and that I still felt something for him. I said I couldn't be with him anymore in light of my feelings because it wouldn't be fair.

"Well, I was definitely not expecting this," he said. "I feel like you just dropped a bomb on me. But OK, I understand. And you're right—it wouldn't be fair to me or to you. As much as it hurts to say, I wish it were another guy for your sake. From what you've told me about him, I think Desmond is a huge jerk."

And to that, I just said, "Thanks for everything, Liam. You're a great person, and I wish you the best. I'm truly sorry," and walked out of his dorm room for the last time.

THIRTEEN

It was Christmas Eve of my sophomore year of college. I was at Aunt Jackie and Uncle Joe's annual Christmas Eve party.

I got a plate of food in the kitchen and brought it to the living room to eat next to Jenna and my brothers and some other cousins. Aunt Jackie and Uncle Joe had just gotten the first floor of the house remodeled into one of those open concepts where the kitchen is only separated from the dining area by an island counter and the dining area and living room spill right into each other, so I could still hear the rest of the family's conversations.

Grandma Vivian helped Grandma Margie put a plate together and sat her at the dining room table between herself and Aunt Linda. My mom was sitting across from them.

"How are you feeling today, Marge?" Aunt Linda asked.

"Just as shitty as ever," Grandma Margie said.

"Oh, Mom, stop. You're having a good day," said Grandma Vivian. "She hasn't had any bathroom troubles, and she ate breakfast *and* lunch today." She spoke in her impressed, upturned tone.

I thought about how much it must bother Grandma Margie that people were conversing about her bowel movements and eating habits right in front of her like she was an oblivious toddler just learning how to shit on a toilet and eat more off her plate than she threw onto the floor. But, on second thought, she was probably having a much worse conversation about them in her head and getting a good laugh from it inside.

"We even went to Mass this evening, so she's been out and about," said Grandma Vivian. "She couldn't miss church on Jesus's birthday."

"I couldn't miss church because your next daddy was there," Grandma Margie said. "I needed to let him get a good look at my legs in this skirt." She kicked one of her legs out from under the table, hiking her just-below-the-knee skirt with a small slit in the side up a few inches to reveal part of her nylon-covered thigh. "I've got to start reeling him in." She winked and giggled girlishly. "You know, church is a great place to meet men," she added, grasping Aunt Linda around the arm.

"I'm not looking. I'm married to your grandson," Aunt Linda answered.

"Well, in case you two don't work out," said Grandma Margie with a shrug.

"Oh, Mother ..." Grandma Vivian said. "Nobody here needs another man, especially you. Don't you think you're too old to be dating?"

"You're never too old to date," said Aunt Linda. "Might as well enjoy the life we have left. Probably won't be very much now for your new fellow." She looked down over her glasses at Grandma Margie. "He doesn't know he's about to hook up with The Black Widow, does he?"

"I give men fair warning," said Grandma Margie. "I say to them, 'Now, do you want to be with me, or do you want to live? Because you can't do both.' I guess for some unlucky souls, life simply isn't *worth* living without me."

"Speaking of dating, Dani got back together with Desmond," my mom said to Aunt Linda.

How predictable, how perfect, I said to myself.

"Really?" said Aunt Linda. "Wasn't she dating someone else?"

"Yes, she was. Seemed like a nice kid too."

Soon, I was being barraged by all my relatives' rather negative opinions about my relationship with Desmond. There was nowhere to take cover from them.

"I thought she was the kind of girl who could tell a guy to kick rocks," I heard my dad say.

I was wounded. I wished I could hole up in my bedroom and sulk. I only felt slightly better after talking to Grandpa Adrian.

"So you got back together with Desmond," he said as I was waiting to take the jug of wine he was filling his glass from to refill my own glass.

"Yeah," I replied sheepishly. He handed me the jug.

"Well, it's your life. No one can tell you how to live it," he said.

Grandpa Adrian became the next center of attention. Uncle Marty tried reasoning with him that he was too old to run the store—he was 10 years older than Grandma Vivian—and should either find someone else to run it or sell it. Then, my uncle attempted to persuade our other relatives to take his side and put more pressure on my grandpa. It was a discussion he brought up a lot, but Grandpa never budged.

I thought the reason no one liked Desmond was because he never came to family things. It would become a catch-22 situation though, because knowing they'd already formed these opinions about him and our relationship, I wouldn't feel comfortable bringing him over anymore. There was a sense of safety in keeping my world with Desmond separate from my family world.

My mom started checking in on me all the time when I went out with Desmond, which was new. She'd call and text asking where we were and what time I planned to come home, and if I didn't respond to her, I'd start getting calls and texts from my dad. It wasn't like we made schedules for our evening plans, so I usually just said that I'd be back "late" or tomorrow.

Knowing my mom had an aversion to me staying out late made it feel like I was sneaking in when I came home at night. I was just as uneasy walking into the house the morning after sleeping at Desmond's, because then my mother would ask why I thought it was OK to do that.

It seemed to me that she believed she could break me and Desmond up again by policing when and how I spent my time with him, and I hated it. I also hated feeling like I was being pushed backward in my life. I'd think to myself, I'm a legal adult and college student, so why am I getting grilled like a high schooler who missed curfew? I was desperately trying to have a sliver of the experience Bernadette, Gabby, Cameron, and all Cameron's cronies were having.

"Anything I choose to do will cause me anxiety," I told Desmond. I was lying with my head in his lap on his bed. "Whether I spend the night or not, I'll feel like a criminal. It's really putting a damper on my evening."

"What do you think about getting our own place?"

I thought of the pain of studying with the TV blaring, the awkwardness of entering the house the morning after a party, of the door handle jiggling, having to worry about being walked in on at the Carveys', and the struggles to retain independence and a college-kid lifestyle when my parents were trying to cut me back down to high school status and undermine my relationship with Desmond.

"I like that idea. Yes. Let's do it," I said.

A month later, we moved into the lower unit of a duplex in the Detroit-Shoreway neighborhood of Cleveland.

Ron told Desmond he needed to take Lee with him and that he was buying Mandy her own puppy, so it was fortunate we found a place that allowed pets.

I left Target for a waitressing job at a bar and grill downtown. I figured that with tips, I could pull in more money than I did in retail. I also got a tutoring job at the writing center on campus. Matt had recommended me to take over his position before he graduated. Between waitressing and tutoring, I was able to split the cost of living evenly with Desmond.

Our unit had two bedrooms. The first was too small for a bed bigger than a twin size, so it became Desmond's studio.

He hung the shelf that he kept his trinkets and little boxes on next to his computer desk again. I suspected he stashed his pills, if he had any, in one of the boxes. I really didn't want to know when or where he had them, but I'd learned that he bought them from Eric's brother Marc.

At this time, Ohio's opioid epidemic was beginning to sound alarms. I'd see advertisements all over on my way to and from school for addiction centers and hotlines and the number of overdose deaths. The number would keep climbing after stronger synthetic opioids, fentanyl and carfentanil, starting spreading through the drug market. By 2017, Ohio would have the second-highest rate of opioid overdose deaths in the U.S., and opioid overdoses would be the leading cause of death for residents under age 55.

In a far corner of my brain, there's a little heap of unobliterated memories from the days in that duplex that I suppose you could call good, and I like to look through them every now and then: staring down at my dirty, white Chucks and holey, dark-wash jeans, my legs across Desmond's lap on the second-hand, velvet, burgundy couch we had in our living room, the walls painted blue-black and dotted with obscure, old paintings and poster art we picked out together at thrift stores and garage sales, Desmond's plastic monster models and my old books on the mantel, a pleasant, perpetual dimness with only lamps and candles for light, which all made the room itself feel like a thrift store or garage sale. Holding hands in Desmond's coat pocket in the biting cold on our way into the local supermarket. Its musky smell. Scrolling through our grocery list on my phone while wearing my black, fingerless gloves, calculating the new total cost of our cart each time Desmond put another item in it to make sure we stayed within budget. Doing my homework at our nicked-up, waxy, wooden dining room table while Desmond cooked dinner and sang along to the songs playing from the speakers in the kitchen, Lee curled up in his bed beside my chair. Warming Desmond's wind-burned cheeks when he came home from work, the smell of outdoors on his clothes and in his hair. Him rubbing my achy legs and feet after my shift at the bar. The clicking of Desmond's mouse and keyboard, the stop and go of instrumentation spilling from his headphones while I sipped tea on the living room window seat, stroking Lee's back with my nails and staring out onto the street—a bunch of sad, crumbling houses, their paint chipping and faded, broken sidewalks, turned harshly uneven by tree roots, the sound of sirens frequent, an uneasiness in the air. But it wasn't my family's street—it was mine—so I thought it was splendid despite the signs of decline. It was romanticized grit that I lived there.

I also lived with depression often, as Desmond and I would cycle back to the same problems, only they'd become worse. I'd see his temper get shorter and shorter, and eventually, he'd explode—sometimes over what seemed to be practically nothing. Once it happened after I dropped a plate of spaghetti.

Desmond had come home from work in a bad mood. He brushed me off when I tried to be affectionate and would hardly speak. I offered to make dinner so he could unwind, but he insisted on doing it.

"Is there *anything* I can do for you?" I asked.

"No. Just do your school stuff," he said.

I worked in the dining room until I saw the food was just about ready. Then I went back into the kitchen.

"Here, let me help you now," I said, pulling plates out of the cabinet. Desmond was wiping off the stove where he'd rested the stirring spoon.

I piled pasta on a plate and set it on the counter, then brought a second plate to the pot on the stove to load that one up. Desmond had started rinsing cookware off in the sink. He didn't like to sit down to dinner until whatever he'd dirtied while cooking was clean.

As I was walking to the counter to set the second plate of spaghetti down and sprinkle parmesan cheese over both of them, Desmond turned around, and I knocked right into him. That's when I dropped the plate, which I guess I hadn't been holding very tightly. Little shards of beige ceramic skated across the floor in every direction.

"Are you fucking kidding me?!" Desmond said. "Perfect. Fucking perfect."

"Relax. It was just a plate," I said.

"Yeah, and now it's just another mess I have to clean up, because you're too fucking stupid to touch something without breaking it."

"*I'll* clean it up, OK?"

"No, don't," said Desmond. "Your dumb ass will probably just break something else."

"Fine," I said. After fixing a new plate, I brought our food and drinks to the coffee table in the living room.

Desmond joined me once he'd finished sweeping up, and I asked what he wanted to watch.

"I don't care," he said, so I put on whatever I was feeling.

I was already done eating, and Desmond had barely picked at his food.

"So you're not eating now?" I said.

"I'm not that hungry at the moment," he answered.

"You've got to be kidding me," I said, rolling my eyes.

"You don't care about anything," I heard him muttering. "You just sit there, stuffing your face, ignoring ..."

I turned up the volume on the TV to drown him out. He grabbed the remote from my hand and threw it at the wall.

"Nice job. Now it's probably broken. But I guess it's OK when *you* break something," I said.

I got up and grabbed my jacket off the back of the dining room chair. I was going to go out for a while to give Desmond a chance to cool down and cool down myself.

"Oh no, you're not walking out of here," Desmond said.

My keys in my pocket, I headed toward the front door anyway. Next I knew, Desmond was wrestling me to the ground. I squirmed and clawed at the floor in an attempt to escape his binding grip around my body. He rolled me over onto my back and pinned down my wrists.

"You're not going anywhere this time. You're stuck with me now. Can't run back to Mommy and Daddy's anymore. They don't want you there."

I strained to wiggle my wrists and kick my legs, hoping it would make him see he should loosen his hold on me, but it only made him press himself into me harder and squeeze my wrists tighter, rubbing them now too to burn my skin.

"Stop moving!" he shouted through clenched teeth. He smacked me hard across my cheek, then regained his grip on the wrist that he'd released momentarily. I began to cry, not even so much because of pain, but from shock.

"Why are you doing this to me?" I sobbed. "I thought you said you were going to work on being better."

"You know what, Dani? I'm sick of you making me feel like I have to work on myself. I'm done tiptoeing around your sensitive little feelings. You think you can do better than me? You think I'm such a bad guy? Wake the fuck up! This is how relationships really are. This is real life. It's not the gingerbread shit in your head. I guarantee even your beloved Grandpa Adrian has slapped your grandma. Get the fuck over it."

I tried wriggling away again.

"I said stop fucking moving!" Desmond yelled. "You're staying right here."

Still holding my wrists, Desmond positioned himself higher up onto my body and dug his knee into the soft tissue on the inside of my bicep. I shrieked, purely from pain this time. Then, Desmond seized my opposite forearm and pulled it back toward his chest as if to perform an arm bar. He added pressure on my elbow joint until he was apparently satisfied with the discomfort he saw in my face, smirking smugly.

"If you move one more time, I swear to god, I'll fucking break it," he said.

"I won't!" I said. He let go of my arm. I choked on a huge sob.

"Stop crying!" he said, hitting me repeatedly in the face and the side of the head. I tried shielding myself with my freed arm, but he pinned it down again with his knee.

The hitting stopped, and I breathed slowly to calm my crying.

"I don't even know why I put up with you sometimes or why I love you, with your sneakiness, your stupidity, your crybaby bullshit. Not to mention the fact that you were with that other guy. You're worthless."

Shortly after we'd gotten back together, Desmond asked if I'd slept with Liam. I told him I had. He was devastated and had to go throw up. It had meant a lot to him to be the only guy I'd slept with, though he'd been with two girls before me. He said they'd just been messing around—that I was the first girl he truly loved, which is why it was so special to him to be my one and only, and he wanted it to stay that way. It took him a while to get past it all and stop bringing it up. During another fight, he said Liam never really cared about me; I was just easy for him since I was vulnerable from our recent breakup.

While he went on belittling me, I began thinking of ways I could catch him off guard and really hurt him so I'd be able to escape.

I could turn and bite his finger or arm, take a chunk of his skin. Then I could gouge his eye, or tear off his ear. My dad had told me it's not hard to do, which is why it's important to wear head gear when grappling.

But is trying to escape too risky? What if my plan fails? What if Desmond gets up faster than I anticipate and catches me or and overpowers me? How badly would he hurt me in retaliation?

As I debated what kind of attack was most likely to be successful, I saw Desmond holding me on the couch while we laughed at an episode of *Friends* I knew he was only watching because I wanted to, us lying in bed on a lazy Sunday morning, kissing passionately, with no other plans for the next several hours but to make love, talk, and kiss some more, recording songs I wrote outside of Ardis Alchemy together in his studio, him cracking me up in the grocery store as he demonstrated his "new walk," consisting of an exaggerated lift on his toes with each step of his front foot, creating a bobbing look, and low-hanging arms with knuckles swinging like an archetypal caveman, which he said he was going to do everywhere he went with me from then on, all our inside jokes, our hands clasped as we strolled through his old neighborhood on a summer night, and I couldn't even hurt him. What a horribly shitty thing it is when your worst enemy is also your best friend.

I stayed there underneath Desmond, unmoving, somber, waiting for him to snap out of the episode he was having. His words were spinning around me like the room does when I wake up still drunk. Eventually, I could no longer comprehend them. I was lost in a fog of fatigue. What came out of his mouth was just sound.

FOURTEEN

After Desmond was done making his point and left me alone, I went to the couch to sleep.

"You're not sleeping on the couch. Come to bed," he said, standing over me.

I didn't want any more trouble; I just wanted to rest, so I followed him to the bedroom. I rolled over as far on my side of the bed as I could without falling off the edge, but Desmond wrapped an arm around my chest and pulled me in close to his body, spooning me, like nothing had happened and all was right between us. His touch was violating and dirty to me. I could only sleep lightly.

It was a relief when Desmond left for work. I had never felt so still as I lay there in our bed alone. The only sound I heard was the pattering of light footsteps above. A single mother lived upstairs with her two young sons. They were probably getting ready for school. The pattering was soothing. It was my rain on the window pane. I turned the alarm on my phone off, resolving that I wouldn't get up for class that day, and finally, I fell into a deep, comfortable slumber.

I started skipping school fairly often as a result of my instability at home and the mental instability it caused me in turn. I figured that as long as I did my assignments and studied, I'd get by just fine.

One professor emailed me out of concern for my frequent absences. I told him I was dealing with a chronic illness. Even if I hadn't been so ashamed of the real reason for missing class, I wouldn't have talked to this professor about it. I didn't trust him. I had him for Political Journalism. He once gave a lesson in which he presented the 9/11 conspiracy theory that the World Trade Center towers were brought down by controlled demolition as fact, though he provided no supporting evidence of it, wrapping up with, "We did it all to ourselves." The students in my proximity appeared eerily undisturbed by his proclamations. I thought, how ironic that a professor who preaches unbiased reporting and truthfulness is force feeding us his own bias. There was no opportunity for debate or questioning. He simply floated on to his next topic of discussion. Case closed.

I woke up just before noon. While in the bathroom, I noticed a rug-burn-looking circle had formed on my cheek. In the evening, I said to Desmond, "Do you see what you did?" pointing it out, and he said, "Come on—that wasn't from me. You did that to yourself in the mirror so you could try to make me feel bad about it."

When I was done examining my face, I decided to take Lee out for a walk. I needed fresh air and sunlight to process and recover from the aftershock of the night before. I remembered overhearing a girl in one of my classes talking about a domestic abuse hotline she worked for. After our walk, I looked it up and called.

A young woman answered the phone. At least I thought she sounded young. Probably not much older than I was, if at all older. I explained that I was calling because my boyfriend had acted out violently toward me and I was hoping they could help in some way.

"So, let me make sure I understand—you live with this boyfriend?" the girl said.

"Yes."

"Have you considered moving out?"

"I honestly can't afford to live on my own right now. I'm a full-time student," I said.

"I see," she answered. "Do you have anyone else you can live with?"

I'm sure Gabby would be OK with it if she didn't live in a dorm. We'd both get in trouble with the university if I got caught staying there long term. I'd probably be a disturbance to my grandparents with my schedule and being out late, and I think there's some truth to what Desmond said about my parents not wanting me in their house anymore.

"I don't think so. Not at the moment," I told the girl. "And see, trying to leave is tricky. That's what got him so angry last night and put me in this situation to begin with."

"You could get a dog," she said.

"A dog?"

"Yes. A dog could guard and defend you."

I looked over at Lee, who was snoozing next to me on the couch.

Not this poor dog.

I had a hard time imagining Desmond being in-hibited by any dog.

"Yeah. Maybe a dog would work. Thanks for your help," I said, trying to end the conversation, because it was clearly no use.

"Of course. I'm always happy to help. Call back any time," the girl said, and I hung up.

My parents both seemed very displeased about me moving in with Desmond. When I announced to them that I was leaving, I felt like they stopped acknowledging me. The most I'd get out of them was a dirty look. It was as though they'd made a plan to give me the silent treatment.

I began staying out even more to avoid the awkward tension. If I had no place to go, I'd often sit in this 24/7 coffee shop in West Park or in my car on some random street.

When I was home, I left my room as little as possible, mainly only to get a drink or food, and even that was hard for me. The day before my move-in date, I crossed paths with my mother in the kitchen—she was looking over some bills at the table—and she said to me, "Do you two actually know how you're paying for everything?"

"Yeah. We both have jobs."

"Do you make enough money at your jobs to afford rent and utilities and food?"

"Yeah, Mom."

"Well, if things get hard to handle, you'll have to live with the choices you've made and figure it out."

"We'll be fine," I said coldly. She's just mad her plan to separate us was a bust.

When Desmond came over to help me get the furniture from my room, my parents carried on as if we were invisible. My mom sat in the dining room reading a book, never looking up from it, and my dad flipped through TV channels in the living room.

My stomach was all in knots the couple times I had to go back to their house to collect some items I forgot. I stayed in my car for several minutes trying to muster up the courage to actually go inside and face them.

I avoided visits to their house from then on. I only came over when I felt obligated to, like on a holiday.

I was even nervous when my parents texted or called. I winced as I opened their texts to full view, and my heart rate increased while I first scanned them for upsetting words.

I usually couldn't bring myself to answer their calls. I'd let the call go to voicemail and listen to the message they left to gauge their tone and find out what kind of conversation I'd be getting into before calling back. They mostly reached out to inform me of an upcoming family gathering.

I was more relaxed around my parents at family gatherings. There seemed enough distractions to take focus off their contempt for me, and I could mostly avoid speaking to them aside from the protocolary greeting, which I'd make phonily chipper, by staying mixed with my other relatives and engaged in conversations with them. If anyone asked a question about Desmond, I'd give a short, vague answer and quickly change the subject.

Nevertheless, I sometimes had too much anxiety to go to family functions at all. I'd become very embarrassed facing the rest of my family members, conjecturing that I was probably one of their gossip topics at home and over the phone and that they thought me to be silly and moronic. As they nodded along to my news telling about school and work and whatnot, I'd worry they were making gibes and laughing at me in their heads, only pretending to take my life happenings seriously.

When I didn't go, I endlessly tried to justify it to myself.

Other college kids aren't expected to come to every little family thing because they're away, so why should I be? I'm very busy. They have too many events.

But no amount of justification ever really eased my mind. I'd be overcome with guilt and wonder if I was resented. I'd feel like I missed out on memories, on catching up on my family's lives. I'm better off though, I'd tell myself. I don't need their judgement and negativity. It's my life, and no one can tell me how to live it! And no one can tell me who to love! Even I can't tell me who to love. Oh, if only I could simply not care what they think or say about me. I don't know why I do.

Days I was particularly anguished over my mixed-emotion familial detachment, I'd take the long way home from school or the bar I worked in to drive by Carmin's. Even a flash of nostalgia as I peeked through the front windows in passing could be such a comfort.

After one of my bar shifts, the store would be closed, but on a day when I didn't have to work after class, I could usually go by Carmin's during business hours. However, my grandpa was only there until 4:00—some of his employees closed shop—so I wouldn't be able to catch a glimpse of him.

One Friday when I wasn't scheduled to work and my afternoon class was cancelled, I decided to stop into the store. I found my grandpa at the deli taking an order from a customer while an employee was hurriedly handing some items over the counter to another customer. I stood away from the counter and waited.

After my grandpa had finished listening to his customer's request, he looked up and spotted me. He appeared taken by surprise, and then his eyes lit up with delight.

"Hey, it's my lovely granddaughter!" he called out, like he was making a store announcement.

"Hi, Grandpa!" I said, stepping closer.

"You here for lunch, sweetheart?" He immediately followed up with, "What do you want?" as if "yes" was the implied answer to the previous question.

"Oh, um …" I hadn't intended to have lunch there. I needed to fill my gas tank, and I wasn't sure I could afford to do that and eat out too. I always came up with my half of the living expenses, but they cost nearly all my earnings. Some days, I had to check my bank account before I bought even a slice of pizza at school.

"How about some lasagna?" Grandpa Adrian said.

At the thought of it, I was warm with nostalgia again. It swelled in my chest.

"That sounds great," I said. Desmond would probably be able to fill my gas tank when he got home if I didn't have the money to.

Grandpa Adrian passed me a tray with a generous portion of lasagna, two slices of garlic bread, and an Italian soda.

"Go sit down, sweetheart. I'll be right over."

"Oh, you don't have to stop what you're doing for me. I know you're busy," I said.

"Nonsense. I've always got time to have lunch with my granddaughter, and it's not often I'm lucky enough to get a surprise visit from her." He winked.

I went up to one of the cashiers to pay. As she started ringing me up, my grandpa yelled, "Donna. Ey, Donna—she's good. No charge."

"Oh," she said, cancelling the tender. "Enjoy." She smiled at me.

I went to one of the little tables lining the front windows and began to eat. I felt so touched, so pathetically destitute, so filled with a sense of loss that a lump formed in my throat and made it hard to swallow my food.

Grandpa Adrian soon joined me.

"So how've you been, Dani?" he asked, searching my face with his eyes.

"Good," I said, which seemed like a lie when it left my lips. "Just busy with school and work and the band." We made some small talk about it all.

"You been over to see your parents lately?" he asked.

"No, not lately," I answered.

"I know college work is tough and time consuming, but I'm sure they miss you."

Doubtful, I thought, staring down into my lap.

"You know," Grandpa Adrian said with a snap of his fingers, his eyes widening, "I might have some ideas for your historical piece." I'd mentioned I was assigned in a journalism class to create a historical narrative of a person, place, or event in Cleveland. We were supposed to pitch three topics to our professor the following week, and I hadn't come up with mine yet. All I knew was that I wanted to write about a place.

"Really?" I said, excited to hear his suggestions and relieved that he wasn't going to persist in discussing my relationships with my parents. I liked that I could still feel safe around him, because he didn't put me on the spot or try to expose me. I liked that when he looked at me, he seemed to see me as he always had.

"You could pitch the West Side Market as a topic. There are vendors who've had their stands for decades you could talk to, and you might be able to find patrons who've shopped there for decades. You could write about Little Italy—the neighborhood as a whole, or a certain restaurant there ... or Alta House, the old social settlement ... you know, John D. Rockefeller started it. Or, you could write about your grandma's department store! The building it used to be in is on the National Register of Historic Places. You'd have your grandmother to interview! She'd love that. Let's see, what else ..."

"Grandpa, say no more—these ideas are great! I'm going to pitch them all!" My imagination was already flurrying with possible content and interview questions.

The professor ended up selecting the department store from my pitches.

My grandpa went on telling stories about times he remembered as a boy and young adult at the West Side Market and in Little Italy. Then he told me about when my grandma ran the department store—how beautiful the store was, how important my grandmother was, how much she loved her career there. I was captivated—taken back to the days when Bernadette and I worked at Carmin's and spent our Friday and Saturday nights sitting at my grandparents' dining room table, just talking with them, and I never wanted to return.

Grandpa Adrian said he had food for me to take home and to come into the kitchen with him to get it. As I watched him moving around the kitchen and deli, packing items up for me in two big paper bags, slicing a loaf of bread to add to one of them, I noticed a fragility about him that I never had before, and it occurred to me that my grandpa, who had always appeared strong and vivacious, taking me to the park and going for evening walks, lifting his dumbbells, working fast-paced all week in the store and still having the energy to entertain a house full of grandkids for the weekend, was getting old. It made me miss him all the more though he was still right there in front of me.

FIFTEEN

Another morning that I decided not to go to class, I took Lee for a long walk in a part of our neighborhood we didn't go to much near an elementary school. I liked changing up our routes for new scenery. We often went to parks or drove to other neighborhoods.

At the end of our walk, we sat on the front steps of a church across the street from the school to bask in the sunlight and warm ourselves. The cool early-spring wind had given me a chill.

I drew in deep breaths, my arms stretched out across my knees and my palms open toward the sky. My gaze wandered from passing cars, to the trees lining the street, to a cardinal flying out of one and perching on the street name sign at the corner of the block, to the carved-in lettering of the school's name above its double doors, and I thought to myself, so many schools I've known are named after men, and so many streets, just as the ones in front of me now. Few bear the name of a woman. I was astonished I never realized it before.

A woman could never run my school or church parish, because only men can make the sacrament of Holy Orders to become part of the church hierarchy. I never questioned it. I guess it became normal to me, as it probably did for everybody I knew.

I felt as though some childhood dream in me had suddenly been extinguished—like I'd just snapped out of a giant illusion I'd lived in all my life, and I was beside myself with disappointment. I was the kid who grew up wanting only to be a solider—all camo pants and mud and tough-kid scowl—but got told they had a disqualification and couldn't be.

Then, I wondered, is the type of relationship I have with Desmond also normal to everyone else? Is he right about that? Has it really been happening all around me my whole life, and I've just been unaware in my idealistic fantasy land? How many of our family members and friends feel and act like Desmond does? You never know what goes on behind closed doors.

Perhaps what Desmond and I have *is* the best I can ever have; I could just keep finding the same thing with other people. A frame of mind like his might be what I need to look past to have the love of a boyfriend, a husband, family—to be able to love them back. Maybe I've made too much of everything with Desmond ... And the more I heard talk of oppression in school and in media, the more these ideas felt validated, and the less control I believed I had over my own life.

I started contemplating what else I'd been wrong about or blind to—like, maybe I'm not really as smart as I think I am. Growing up, everybody always told me I was smart because I got good grades, but it probably wasn't such a hard thing to do in a Catholic school without the resources to keep challenging students and fewer students to challenge each other. I took what people said about me for granted. I hadn't considered that I might not have what it takes to be who I want to be. I could end up a complete loser. I mean, what have I even achieved so far in my life? What do I have to show for myself in all this time I've been in the world?

I'd always be mentally listing off what I saw as my biggest accomplishments in an attempt to convince myself of my life's value, but it was never any consolation.

Maybe you're not that pretty either, I'd say to myself. Just because Desmond finds you attractive doesn't mean other men will. *Most* men might not find you attractive.

What if a lot more guys are bothered by my height than I thought, and they don't classify me as "curvy," but simply, fat? And what if more guys than I realize still see my hair as a hideous frizz ball? What if Desmond and I split up, and I never find another man who thinks I'm as beautiful as he does?

Sometimes, I'd look in the mirror and try to pinpoint exactly what made my face ugly. It's too asymmetrical. My eyes are too small. My forehead is kind of big. My nose is too long, too pointy. I wish I had poutier lips. And stronger cheekbones—they'd probably help my face look slimmer. My skin is too shiny, and it's so pale that it's probably jarring to people. I bet they think I look sickly. I don't have that tanning-salon "healthy glow" I'm told is to be desired. My ears are oddly shaped. Really, my entire face is oddly shaped.

There isn't a little fix that will make it better. Why would anyone want me?

I couldn't believe how I used to just skip through life when I was younger like I had it all and everything was so fucking great. Who did I think I was? I didn't know who I was at all anymore. I was certainly not the same girl who dreamed of being president.

I still went to the 24-hour coffee shop in West Park sometimes—I'd work on school assignments there when I felt like getting out of the dining room—but it became difficult to be in the coffee shop on busy evenings. The space between me and every person who passed by was like a magnifying lens, intensifying my inadequacies, my loneliness, my anxiety.

Whenever someone looked at me, I'd flinch, as I was sure they were thinking I'm ugly, I'm weird, pathetic, that I probably have no friends and nobody loves me, I'm stupid, I'm generic, I'm trash. My heart sounded in my ears, the ticking of the time bomb I was.

From the window where I'd sit with my laptop, I'd watch the little groups coming out of the Irish pubs across the street—holding hands, blowing cigarette smoke, laughing so hard that they tipped forward and nearly toppled over each other onto the sidewalk. The more fun they looked like they were having, the worse I felt. I'd think, they seem so happy—they must have things I don't. I wish I had enough to be happy. I wish I was enough to be happy.

I'd wait until all the bars closed down and the street emptied out before walking to my car to go home. Desolate as I was, it was a relief when there was no one to see me.

SIXTEEN

When Bernadette came home for spring break junior year, she invited me on a four-day trip to a cabin that belonged to the family of one of her high school friends. It was in southeastern Ohio, just a hop, skip, and a jump away from West Virginia.

"I'm really over the whole Florida spring break deal," she told me. "It's just so much chaos. Something chill sounds way better."

I uttered some words of agreement though I hadn't known the Florida spring break thing was actually all that common. I thought it was MTV's inflation of reality, being so far from my own reality at the time.

We took Bernadette's car, a Corolla she bought used in high school and kept at her parents' house while she was away at college.

"Hmm, what driving tunes should we put on?" Bern asked once we'd gotten on the highway. "Ah, I know!" she answered before I had time to ponder it. Her pick was "Meatballing Music."

"It's been a long time since I've played this," she said.

"Me too."

Listening to the lyrics for "Chapel of Love," I had to turn toward the window and squint really hard at the trees in the distance to keep from crying. I could no longer bear such blissful, romantic notions. How they teased me, like an uncatchable butterfly, flaunting beauty and perfection that seemed would forever be out of my reach. Thinking on the song, it was amazing to me that ones like it were ever written in that period. Tumultuous relationships are all too common now, and back then, they could have only occurred even more commonly, I concluded. The romance of the era was probably a façade.

I wondered how many of the musicians and other artists I'd admired all my life saw women as inferior, smacked their wives or girlfriends around. That was when I stopped putting people on pedestals. I realized if I did, they'd almost certainly be torn down from them, discredited, and hated for one reason or another, for standards of moral purity are impossible for humans to live by, and our minds continually evolve, redefining morals anyway. People's inability to accept this surprises me more than any transgressions.

The stories of human history are as brutal as the wild predator shows on National Geographic. The blood running through us comes from people who, in this day and age, we'd want locked up for their barbarism—a truth that nobody on Earth is exempt from, not that we choose our ancestors anyway—and, conversely, from people who were imprisoned and even executed in their time for things that are only minor offenses now, or not ones at all.

People famous for their important contributions to society, clergy members who've fed the poor and tended to the sick and taught about virtues, have also done dishonorable things. And so I'd rather not let someone's personal mistakes or unpopular opinions negate their great work; what would be left to enrich us if the value of every piece of work were based solely on the mutable merit of its creator's character rather than the merit of the work itself?

How we've become a society that offers forgiveness and reintegration assistance to those formerly incarcerated for violent crimes but demands those whose worst offenses are words be ostracized or their work abolished baffles me.

A little over an hour into the drive, Bernadette's car started making a revving sound, and the speedometer dropped to zero. After another 10 minutes of the revving and the speedometer jumping all over the place, Bern was too freaked out to keep going.

We took the next exit for Schmidtville and pulled into a big gravel lot just past the town's welcome sign to park. On the side of the lot opposite us was a gas station. The only other thing within it was a sign for a restaurant that had apparently been razed, stating, "BREAKFAST ALL DAY" and "PIE $3.00."

Bernadette decided to call her mom about the car trouble. The bars on her phone were so low that she kept having breakup. I thought, worse comes to worst, we can see if the gas station has a phone, and maybe I could get some gum and a tea, but after a second look, I discovered that the gas station had been abandoned.

The rest of our surroundings were fields still tinged brown from frost, a hillside of bare trees, which I thought was probably quite pretty when the leaves returned or covered in fresh snow, an old brown barn faded to a near gray that seemed it could collapse with a strong wind, and a few dingy houses with rusted-out cars and heaps of other rusty and broken things next to their porches.

Bern's mom told her to contact roadside service, so she did, but of course, the call dropped. She put her head on the steering wheel and groaned in frustration.

"Maybe we should get out of the car and try to find a spot with a better signal," I said.

"Yeah, that's probably a good idea," said Bern. "And if we can't, we could go inside the gas station and ask if they have a phone."

"I'm thinking they won't."

She looked over at the gas station quizzically and then started laughing this laugh where her shoulders shrug. She always laughed that way when seeing the comedy in the misfortunes we faced together.

So we got out of the car and, thankfully, found an area where Bernadette had enough bars to keep a connection.

As she arranged for a tow, I kicked around the ground in small circles and peered at the assortment of bike parts, old toys, and rocking chairs in one house's junkyard. I thought about how nice it would be to live someplace like this, away from the rest of the world, rid forever of the family or anyone else who judged me. To have no one to please, no one to impress, no one to compete with, no one to miss, and to expel media, pop culture, and all the reminders of things that made me ill with anger and hopelessness. When a person decides they're done with the narcissism and insanity of society and to cancel their membership for it, scrap its frivolous merch, I bet this is where they come. Makes good sense. Maybe here, I'd finally find peace and die happy.

I picked up a stone at my feet and went to the welcome sign, where, beneath the part that read, "Welcome to Schmidtville," I etched, "A Wonderful Place To Die." I giggled fiendishly to myself as I stood back to inspect my work. Bern didn't notice what I'd done, as she was preoccupied with trying to help the service rep identify our location.

The friend who invited Bernadette was nice enough to meet us and bring us to the cabin himself. He ended up driving us home too, since he was going back to his parents' house in the Cleveland area after our little retreat.

Our days in Appalachia weren't exactly "chill." There was a fairly large group of people, lots of drinking and smoking around a bonfire, blasting music, and shooting off fireworks. Bern seemed to enjoy herself nonetheless.

As far as the eye could see were jagged, thickly-wooded hills. It felt possible that they went on forever, that nothing and no one existed but them and us, and that was the only aspect of the trip I smiled genuinely about. The rest of the time, I talked and observed from behind a mask with a painted-on smile so I wouldn't embarrass Bernadette or put a damper on her fun, acting as though the conversations I was holding, the experience we were having, and life itself interested me at all.

SEVENTEEN

It was a day in the beginning of my senior year. I was supposed to get up earlier than usual so I could stop at the pharmacy to get my birth control before my shift at the writing center, because the pharmacy would be closed when I got off work at the restaurant. I woke up later than I should have, leaving no time to make breakfast or coffee. I'm irritable without them. I forgot that I needed to put gas in my car until I was behind the wheel. That was going to make me even later. Then, the tech at the pharmacy counter told me my insurance company wouldn't cover the birth control.

"This again?" I groaned. They'd done this to me before. "I don't understand—it's covered by my plan," I said.

"It requires prior authorization," said the tech.

"What does that mean?" I whined this time, rolling my head back like I was about to throw myself on the floor and have a two-year-old-style tantrum.

"It means your physician needs to speak with your insurance provider to get approval for the prescription before they'll cover it."

"But didn't they already do that?"

"It probably has to be done every time your prescription is refilled," she said.

"That's ridiculous. How will I know if my doctor has talked to them? Does she even know she's supposed to talk to them?"

"You can give your doctor a call, or we can call if you'd like."

"Really? You'll do that?" I said.

"Yes, we can."

"That would be helpful. Thank you. How will I know when it's approved?"

"We'll call you, but if it makes you feel better, you can keep checking in with us each day to see where we are in the process. If you really need the prescription now, you can still have it. It's just that it'll be the full price of $50."

I'd need it the next day, when I was to start a new pill pack, but I couldn't bring myself to pay $50 for it when it'd normally only cost a fraction of that, especially when I was so broke.

"I'll come back for it," I said glumly.

"OK," said the tech with a better-luck-next-time look on her face. It infuriated me that her reaction to this predicament was so disproportionate to mine.

Birth control was one thing Desmond wouldn't help me pay for. His reasoning was that I'd be on it regardless of if we were together because I'd be sleeping with someone else.

When I arrived for my shift at the writing center, I realized I didn't have my phone. I thought I tossed it in my bag as I was scrambling to get out the door, but, apparently, I had not. I hoped Desmond would find it when he got off work so he'd understand why I was unresponsive all day.

Katrin had also gotten a job there. She sat at the table across from mine looking over papers for her boyfriend, Jordan, and Persuasive Essay Girl, whose name I'd learned was Patrice—they'd become friends I guess.

After Katrin finished up with her edits, Patrice asked, "So are we still on for Saturday?"

"Yeah," Katrin and Jordan both answered, nodding in affirmation.

"OK. Did we ever decide what we're doing?" said Patrice.

"No," sighed Katrin. "I want to go someplace off campus. I'm just not sure where."

"We could go see the river that caught on fire," said Jordan.

"Why would anyone want to go see that?" Katrin said.

"Because it's probably the most notable thing that ever happened here," he said.

"I'm good on that," said Katrin, "but if you want to go on your own, knock yourself out."

"I was making a joke, obviously," he said, playfully elbowing her.

I chimed in, "That happened decades ago. The river is way healthier now, if you *did* actually want to see it. People boat and paddle board on it. And cities across the country used to catch fire all the time before more legislation was passed for environmental protections. The media just chose to blow up the story about our river."

None of them responded. Patrice raised an eyebrow and smirked slightly.

"How about the Cleveland Zoo?" Patrice said. "I'm sure it doesn't compare to the zoo at, like, Disney, but I think it'll still be fun. My family went to Disney's Animal Kingdom all the time when I was a kid. It's one of the best zoos in the country."

"We used to always visit the San Diego Zoo," said Katrin. "It's also said to be one of the best in the country. I love, *love* San Diego. I really miss it."

"Why did you move to Northeast Ohio anyway?" Patrice said.

"My dad's company transferred him here," Katrin replied.

"Must have been a demotion," said Patrice with a cynical laugh. "I'm sorry for you. Do you like Maine, Jordan?"

"Yes, I do. It was a beautiful place to grow up with the ocean and the mountains right there," he said.

"Are you going to go back?" said Patrice.

"I don't know where I'll be going yet. Maybe to California." He gazed into Katrin's eyes like they held his future.

"Or how about Seattle, or Portland? Or maybe Brooklyn?" said Katrin, mirroring Jordan's look.

"Anywhere is better than here," Patrice said.

Figures Jordan and Katrin would only name places on the coasts, I thought. I can see them in a hipster apartment in one of those areas. Media mostly forgets about the space between the coasts, and so other people do as well. Feels like Middle America is acknowledged by the media only to reinforce the image they've created of it as a cesspool, with inhabitants inferior to the coasts' in all ways, each of us a disease that needs eradicated from the nation. They accomplish this through scorn, mockery, and the telling of biased, unbalanced narratives. The sanctimonious assholes who spread the hate, lies, and negative stereotypes have probably never even been here. They don't have a clue.

Patrice, who'd been intermittently people watching out of the writing center's glass windows as the three of them chatted, then said, "And you know something? I've noticed there are more trashy people here than in other places. Have you guys noticed that?"

Being fed up with the day as it was, I felt I had no grace left with which to coolly bear such disparagement, and so I was not at all inhibited to say, "If you all hate this area so much, why are you here? I'm sure your mommies and daddies would have paid for you to go anywhere you wanted. Oh, was it because you couldn't get in anyplace else but this shitty school in our lowly little town?"

That shut them all up, and Patrice and Jordan left the writing center just minutes after. I smiled inwardly and congratulated myself on coming up with such a clever and effective counterattack.

As I sat waiting for the professor to come into one of my classes later, I couldn't help but be distracted by two girls whispering and giggling while stealing glances at me. One started letting her gaze linger on me audaciously, as if she wanted me to know she was talking about me. Feeling I was the butt of some cruel joke, for which I couldn't think of the slightest reason why, I turned my most intense glare on them. The girl who'd been taking the longer looks at me noticed first. Her expression completely changed from amused to frightened. She nudged her friend in alarm, like I might be about to do something crazy, and I liked it. I felt so wonderfully sick, ablaze with fury and ruthlessness. I held my menacing stare until the professor began her lecture.

When I came home from the restaurant that night, I found my phone sitting on the dining room table and Desmond working in his studio. I said hi to him. He greeted me with only a solemn nod.

Seeing he was in a mood, I decided not to bother trying to talk anymore and went to the kitchen for a snack. I made a peanut butter and jelly sandwich and was rinsing some grapes in the sink when I heard him throw something in the studio and curse. Then, he came out into the kitchen.

"Something bothering you I take it?" I said to him.

"Yeah, a lot of things are bothering me. My day has been fucking fantastic. One of the things bothering me has to do with you. Want to tell me who Nate is?"

"What?" I said, my stomach getting fluttery at the feeling of an imminent fight.

"You left your phone on the table, and I saw a couple of your texts. Someone named Nate asked if you're free next Friday because he got tickets to a comedy show."

"He works at the restaurant," I said. "We exchanged numbers in case we need to trade shifts. He asked a few days ago if I'd consider switching shifts with him if he ended up getting some comedy show tickets, and I told him I'd think about it."

"Mhmm. You're sure the tickets weren't for the two of you to go on a date?"

"Don't be ridiculous. I'm positive. Did you go through my phone?"

"I don't need to when your messages pop up on your screen. Is there a reason you don't want me going through it?"

"No," I said. "Would I have given you the passcode if there was?" I'd let him have it a long time ago to show I had nothing to hide.

"Then why did you sound so defensive when you asked if I went through it? And why do you care if I did? Am I not allowed to now?"

I was checked out of the conversation, because I figured anything I said would just make Desmond want to argue. I took my food to the couch and put my tired feet on the coffee table.

"Hey, I wasn't done talking to you!" said Desmond, shoving my feet off the tabletop.

The bold relentlessness I had that day still rested upon my shoulder. I said, "Well I was done talking to you." I kicked my feet back up and took a bite of my sandwich. Then, Desmond decided to flip the table.

In the back of my mind, I knew attempting to leave only ever stoked his anger more, but instinctually, I went for my keys. He tried to take them away, twisting my wrist as I resisted giving them up and hitting me in the side of the head.

When I realized I'd lost too much of my grip to be able to free the keys from him, I let go and made a sprint to the far door in our hallway that we never used. Behind it was a stairwell to the upstairs unit. I ran up the steep, wooden steps, yelling for help in hopes that the woman who lived there would let me in. The sound of my voice echoing through the stairwell surprised me. It was like it was coming out of someone else. I guess it was just that I never fathomed begging a stranger to help me.

I continued calling out as I pounded on my neighbor's door, but no one opened it. Desmond started muscling me back down the steps. I managed to squirm away briefly and reclimb a few steps on my hands and knees, but then Desmond grabbed ahold of my ponytail, and in a clunking, scraping, bruising manner, dragged me down again. In a last-ditch effort to get my neighbor's attention, I screamed like a girl in a horror movie.

"If you don't shut the hell up, this will be the last night you ever live. I'll fuckin' bury you. Then I'll murder your whole family," Desmond said.

He pulled me all the way into our bedroom before he unclenched my hair enough that I could get myself off the floor. He posted up against the door to make sure I wasn't able to try leaving this time.

With my adrenaline so high that I was seeing spots and nowhere to flee, I did something I never dreamed I would: I threw a punch at Desmond—a straight right—catching him square in the jaw. He put his hand to his face, appearing taken aback, and so I took the opportunity to hit him again—this time with a jab to the chin. I knew my fists would not deter him, but I also knew that turning the other cheek as I always did wouldn't either. I'd be hurt regardless, so I wanted Desmond to be hurt too for once.

As I watched him roll his tongue over his front teeth to check their condition, my mind started reeling with worse things I could do, like hit him over the head with the lamp from my dresser, or use the heel of one of my pumps to dig into a number of places. You can't take that long to think about it though, so being ambivalent, I impulsively swung at Desmond again. He anticipated it and was able to block me. In light of this, for some reason, I spat on him.

"You worthless fucking cunt," he said, wiping the spit from his chin. In a flicker, his hands were around my throat, and he was pushing me onto the bed. Then he was pressing a pillow into my face. I kicked him mercilessly and thrashed about. He yelped once and suddenly got up. I threw the pillow to the floor. He put his hand over his eyes, took a deep breath, and walked out of the room.

I sat on the bed for a long time. Finally, Desmond came back. He didn't step past the doorway.

"I'll be sleeping on the couch," he told me.

"OK," I said. After he went away, I locked the bedroom door.

EIGHTEEN

Before I was fully awake the next morning, I could already feel the deep depression crushing my lungs. It crept through the first inkling of consciousness like a morning-after regret. Fortunately, it was Saturday, and I had no plans, so it wasn't necessary to leave my bed.

I eventually got up to unlock the door and poke my head out to hear what Desmond was up to. I didn't hear anything. I lay back down, and what could have been half an hour or an hour and a half later—it's tough to judge while remaining still and staring at the insides of your eyelids—I felt Desmond come into the room. He started changing his clothes quickly and quietly.

"Are you going somewhere?" I said.

"Yeah, to Eric's. I left a note. I didn't want to wake you." He gently pushed some hair back from my eyes. "I made you some breakfast too. It's in the microwave."

"When will you be back?"

"I'm not sure. Probably late. I might stay over. I'll let you know." He kissed my forehead and was gone.

The note was taped to the microwave door. It read that he was going to Eric's, would let me know if he was staying, was sorry he let things get so out of hand the night before, and that he hadn't meant the awful words he said.

I decided to draw myself a bath. When the water had cooled to an uncomfortable temperature and my fingers and toes had long been pruned and I really wanted to get out, I couldn't. The weight in my chest made it too hard to stand. I inched my fingers along the side of the tub until they were resting upon the ledge. I grasped the ledge tighter and used it as an anchor to pull my body close enough that I could lift my elbows onto it. With my elbows, I hoisted myself into a sitting position on the side of the tub. Then, I swung my legs over, one at a time, onto the bath mat. Each step of getting ready for the day was slow and painful like this, and so it took almost the entirety of it.

I'd come to understand what it was like to need something to dull the pain—to get through. I was curious how it might feel to try some of the pills Desmond took.

I thought, I could go snooping in the boxes on his shelf, see if he currently has any I can snatch. That would save me the trouble of seeking someone out to buy them from. But Desmond might keep count of his pills. Yes, he probably does. He'd notice they're missing. To be safe, I should just drink.

I went out to one of the bars in West Park near the 24-hour coffee shop. Although I was very insecure around other people, I thought the energy of a crowd might do me some good. The fallout I was having from that fight felt like the worst one ever. I needed a glimpse of my former state of normalcy. I'd start experiencing this inner conflict a lot of wanting to be completely isolated but also wanting company. You're a walking contradiction, I'd tell myself. There's so much contradiction crammed into your short little body that it's a wonder you haven't exploded yet.

This particular bar is open as a family restaurant during the day, and the Moran side often had gatherings there when I was young. The owner back then knew us each by name. It's always been a staple of the neighborhood—the epitome of what the neighborhood aspires to be in spirit. It's somewhere I know I can always belong if I want to, despite having tried most of my life not to belong in the typical West Park spots.

As expected, I saw some familiar faces immediately upon walking inside. It was two of my father's school buddies first.

"Hey, it's Billy's daughter. Billy Moran," the guy I knew better said to the other, nodding toward me. I smiled at them.

My dad's parents and three of his siblings—he was one of six—stayed in West Park. It's common to find multiple generations of a family living within streets of each other in the area.

It felt like everyone I met in West Park had a connection to my dad or his family—the parents of my classmates, the school librarian, the pharmacist at the corner drug store, the mail man. Pick a random person off the street there, and I'd bet that I could link them to the Morans. Grandma Celia, my dad's mom, loved finding the link between us and anybody that we mentioned was also from West Park. One *always* turned up if she dug deep. "Yes, your boyfriend's grandpa went steady with my cousin's best friend's sister," she might conclude. Or, "Your softball coach's mom was the babysitter of our neighbors three houses down. Nice girl. Nice family." Always nice if they were from our neighborhood. And if they were also Catholic, as so many in the area are, we were practically related. Her associations with Catholics went beyond West Park. She believed she knew every Catholic in Greater Cleveland one way or another.

On the other side of the circular bar, I spotted a few guys from Holy Rosary and a married couple who lived on my parents' street. I wondered if the couple or my dad's old school friends would mention they saw me. I sort of hoped they would.

When I sat down, I noticed a girl from Holy Rosary was bartending—Meghan Flannery. She was someone I wished to never run into again for the rest of my life, so it was a bit shocking and uncomfortable to see her there.

Bernadette and I only had a few other close friends in grade school. Perhaps it was partially because our bond with one another was so strong that we didn't have a great need for many friends, and I had cousins who I hung out with regularly anyway, but by seventh grade, it was mainly, undeniably, because we were a different type than the majority of the Holy Rosary girls. They were the UGG boots, Abercrombie, bob-wearing, basic preps, and their musical palates were limited to the five songs being played over and over again on the hits station that week. We were the Doc

Martens, thrift-store flannels, long-haired, mosh-pit music lovers. We didn't want to mingle with them as much, if not more, than they didn't want to mingle with us.

I'd thought Meghan was a bratty crybaby in grade school, and though she was on the quieter side, she liked to snap at other kids with cruel and aggressive remarks for no reason. We had our share of unfriendly exchanges in the bathroom and locker room, initiated by her. My aunt was one of her mom's best childhood friends, which made her displaced anger toward me all the more frustrating. And she had this friend named Riley who, while not very mean, would irk me with these idiotic statements about wanting things that are generally undesired by the rest of society—like, "Braces look so cool. I wish I had braces." In my head, I was like, yeah, the pain of shifting teeth that makes your jaw feel locked as tight as a bear trap and your face feel like it's been beaten with a brick is so glamorous, as is having chunks of everything you eat get stuck in your brackets so that you either have to be that nerd who brushes their teeth after lunch every day or go without food until you're home from school. I would know, as someone who had braces.

Another time, she said, "Man, I wish I didn't have 20/20 vision so I could get glasses too." Because it's so overrated to see everything clearly simply by opening your eyes. She also said she wanted to have acne because using Proactiv "seems like fun."

While spacing out during the homily at a school Mass one day, I made up a plot for an episode of *The Twilight Zone* based on the things she said. Teenagers were lathering their faces at night with a dirty oil from a bottle that promised "increased white heads, papules, and nodules in just 3 days!" and "produces redness and shine." There were ads on Google for a capsule form of flu germs. One of them read, "Do you have the latest strand of the flu yet? Get it now!" All the cool kids were staying home sick. And there was an infomercial selling diet pills to help you reach your fat gain goals.

Meghan also went to St. Ambrose. Luckily, I only had one class with her in our four years there, and our lockers were never in close proximity.

She came over to me at the bar to take my order.

"Hi, Dani," she said. "What can I get for you?"

I was surprised she used my name. I was expecting her to act as if she'd never seen me before.

I got a vodka tonic with lime. Cupping the glass in both my hands, I took heavy sips of it like it was a healer for the soul akin to herbal tea or chicken noodle soup.

I did not feel good at all about retaliating against Desmond. It had been gratifying in the moment, but in retrospect, I was absolutely disgusted, nauseated from self-loathing. No longer was I the righteous, merciful one between us in my mind, or the least bit fit to try to save him. I was filthy, foul. I couldn't believe how easily I'd crossed the line. I guess it had become too blurred for me to see it.

Profanity, in songs, is art. Used by our friends, it's cool and funny. Coming from your partner, it's hurtful. Violence, in sports, is often encouraged, and sanctioned. In film, it's glorious; beating, killing, raping. People can't get enough. In consensual rough sex, violence is playful, thrilling. But, in a lover's real anger …

I wanted to puke and puke until I had literally puked my guts out, start over empty, rid of all the rottenness that became beneath my flesh.

Or has it always existed deep within me, and Desmond is a magnet for it, pulling it to the surface?

I might be just as guilty as he is now. Maybe I evened the score, or am at least catching up, and I deserve all the shit he gives me, and all the worst things life gives me.

I imagined the vodka to be cleansing me internally as it burned down my throat. I hoped enough of it would incinerate all my thoughts.

I rested my elbows on top of the bar and twisted the Claddagh ring I wore on my right ring finger around and around. It was my favorite ring, a gift from Grandma Celia when I made my Confirmation. The band, hands, and crown were silver, and the heart was a yellow-gold encased ruby. My grandma said she picked that one because she loved red on me most. I like it most on myself too. I'd had the heart facing in for so long.

A man suddenly sat down on the stool next to me. His slightly tangled hair fell to his shoulders. He had a thick beard and wore a beanie, and he looked to be somewhere between his late twenties and early thirties.

"Hi, I'm Greg," he said. I said hi and returned to brooding over my drink. I instinctively looked back at him a few minutes later due to the weight of his stare, which prompted him to ask, "What's your name?"

I hesitated at first but still gave him my real name.

He attempted small talk, asking me a series of trivial questions about myself. I never detested small talk as much as most people say they do, but this small talk couldn't be brought to a close in the usual fashion with one individual needing to go abruptly to catch a bus or a plane or be seen for an appointment, and I was uneasy about where it was heading.

When I was almost finished with my drink, Greg bought me another.

"I should tell you—I have a boyfriend," I said to him.

"I don't care," he said with a shrug. I wasn't sure how to take that. I thought, does he not care because buying me a drink is only a friendly gesture with no ulterior motive involving sexual favors, or does he not care in the sense that he has no reservations about trying to be with someone who's already taken or regard for how I might feel about him doing so?

"So what do you do?" he said as I took a sip.

"I'm a student. I work part-time as a waitress and a tutor." I replied. "What do you do?"

He squinted up at the ceiling like he was contemplating something. Finally, he said, "I haven't worked a regular job in a long time."

"What does that mean?" I asked. "Do you sell drugs or something?" Meghan, who was mixing a drink nearby, started eyeballing him. She must have overheard.

Greg smiled as if my question had been a joke and went on gulping his beer until it was nearly gone. Then he said, "Next round's on you."

"Uh, is it? I don't remember offering to buy. That's going to be a negative." I certainly didn't have money to waste on his drinks.

"All right. Touché. But then to be fair ..." He slid the drink he bought me from out of my hand toward himself.

A moment later, he said, "I'm just kidding. You can keep it," and he pushed the drink back to me.

I said, "It's fine—you didn't need to buy it for me in the first place. You can have it if you want. Really." He shook his head.

"Well, thanks, I guess." As I looked away in discomfort, I saw Meghan watching him again.

"So, you want to get out of here soon?" said Greg.

"No. No, I don't," I answered. "I'd like to stay right here."

"My place isn't far from here at all," he said in a reassuring tone, as if that was all I should need to hear to be convinced.

I ignored him and started looking around for Meghan so I could close my tab. I didn't actually want to leave yet, but more than that, I didn't want to be stuck with him anymore. I was relieved to catch Meghan's eye quickly. She approached us, and before I had a chance to ask for my check, she said to Greg, "I think someone is looking for you out on the patio."

"What? Who?" he said.

"I don't know," said Meghan. "I didn't see them. One of the barbacks told me the description they gave sounded like you, and isn't your name Greg?"

"Yeah," said Greg, looking worried.

"Seems urgent. You better go check it out."

Greg stood up and patted his pockets down, checking to make sure he had all his belongings I supposed.

"Do you want to close your tab now? It's probably a good idea," said Meghan.

"Sure," he replied.

We watched him leave after he signed his check.

"Did you just make all that up?" I said to Meghan.

"Yeah." She laughed. "You looked cornered. He comes in here every now and again. He's always seemed questionable to me."

"I appreciate your help. Thank you," I said.

"In case he comes back, here—" she pulled a purse out from behind the bar. "Put this on the stool and act like your friend is sitting there. Don't let anyone steal it though. It's mine."

"I won't."

A couple minutes later, Greg came back.

"Excuse me. Excuse me, miss," he called over the bar. Meghan turned around and lifted her eyebrows at him in that way to say, "Yeah?"

"I didn't find anyone looking for me outside," said Greg.

"Huh—that's strange. I don't know what to tell you," she said.

Greg looked at the stool he'd been sitting on, now with the purse resting there.

"Sorry—your seat's been taken by my friend," I said to him. He shifted his eyes, seeming suspicious and annoyed, then turned and left for good.

Meghan gave me a wink, and I smiled at her, slurping up the last drops of my free drink. I bought another and another and another. I can afford it tonight, I told myself. I need it tonight. I'll be more frugal with meals next week to compensate.

Perhaps Meghan isn't so bad anymore after all. It could be possible that we'd even like each other now. She had obviously let go of whatever grudge she'd been holding against me all those years ago. How immature am I for not letting go of it, or the little differences between us, like our fashion sense and taste in music? Some things are bigger than our differences I guess.

By 1:30, I knew I was way past my limit to be able to drive. I was having to mentally walk myself through unzipping my jeans and turning on the faucet at the sink in the bathroom like they were new concepts, which is always a sure sign to that tiny fiber of clarity holding on somewhere deep in my brain that I'm far gone. This was just before Uber and Lyft became hugely popular, and taxis in Cleveland were and still are basically non-existent, so I was beginning to grow a bit nervous, realizing I'd be having one of those paranoid drives home; you know, where you try not to do anything clumsy that gives you away, such as drive outside the lines, and also not do anything that appears unnaturally compliant with traffic laws like you've got something to hide—for instance, drive under the speed limit—all the while constantly looking out at your sides and in your rearview mirror for inconspicuous cop cars, so your eyeballs are moving in this manic, clock-like way: road, speedometer—don't drive too fast, don't drive too slow—right, rear, left, repeat.

Desmond texted to see what I was doing. I told him I was at the bar, drunk. He insisted on picking me up and coming back for my car in the morning. I said OK and agreed to meet him in the parking lot out back, and I was immediately angry at myself for it.

Here you go again, falling right back into him. Love is a big, fat, fucking bully. I want to swing a metal baseball bat into its gut.

There was always something to be angry about—my dependency on Desmond, my crumbling relationships with my family, my financial situation, my perceived inadequacy, the feeling that nobody liked or understood me, or anyone or anything else in this entire part of the country, especially my city, the restraints I believed society was keeping on me. How I wished I could clench the world in both my fists and bust it like a water balloon.

I spotted three empty beer bottles along the front of a dumpster in the parking lot. I picked one up and chucked it across the blacktop. I felt a snapping within me as the bottle turned to shards, like it had happened inside my body. It was satisfying. I threw another.

I started toying with the idea of chucking the last one through the back window of a shop that was for sale a couple buildings down. How would breaking glass with glass feel? I wondered, rubbing my thumb over the threading on the neck. I held the bottle out over my view of the window and tried to judge if I could make the throw from where I was standing.

The bottle and the window became illuminated by headlights. I turned in the direction of the lights and found Desmond pulling up.

"What are you doing?" he said through his rolled-down window, looking concerned. "Were you going to throw that?"

I put the bottle on the ground and rolled it away with my foot. Then I got into the car.

"You realize that breaking something with a beer bottle would be vandalism and that you could be charged with a felony for it, right?" said Desmond.

Says a guy who does all kinds of things that could be felonies. Hypocrite.

"I mean, I've damaged some property before, but that was when I was a kid. You're too old to be able to get away with it as easily as I did," he added.

Yeah, you're too old for this teenage angst, Dani Moran. You're supposed to be grown and figured out and getting established and shit. So what are you going to do? What will become of you?

I thought the nausea would go away in the weeks that followed as things between me and Desmond simmered down again, but it didn't. In fact, it started to get worse. On top of it, I was becoming increasingly fatigued. At first, I didn't think much of the fatigue, because it had always been my body's response to stress and depression, but then, my breasts began to hurt too. They throbbed so badly at night that I was often awakened from my sleep. I started panicking. What if I'm sick, I thought? Could these be signs of breast cancer? I examined myself, but both my breasts had grown so swollen that I couldn't distinguish between normal tissue and lumps. Wait … could it be? Pregnancy? Impossible—I've been on birth control for years. What are the chances, like, one in 100?

I got a box with two pregnancy tests in it and took each at home when Desmond was at work. They were both positive.

NINETEEN

Later that day, after Desmond finished dinner, I said, "I need to talk to you about something."

"All right. What's going on?" he said.

"You know how I told you I've been feeling strange? I thought maybe I should take a pregnancy test. I took two of them, and both were positive. I still have them in the bathroom if you care to see."

I braced myself for his reaction. It was boggled eyes and one hard blink.

"How is this possible? You're on birth control," he said.

"I thought the same thing, but remember when I had to wait to get my birth control because of that problem with my insurance?"

"Yeah, but you got it only a couple days later than you needed it, and you still took all the pills."

"Well, apparently being a couple days late, even when you take the pills you missed, is enough to do it," I said. "I didn't think I was ovulating. I guess I don't really know how to figure out when I'm ovulating.

I thought I did, but obviously I was wrong, or the rhythm method I was basing my ovulation schedule on is wrong. At least for me. My body must have its own weird rhythm or something. But, you know what? I've heard you never ovulate while on birth control. Technically, you never get a period either. It's withdrawal bleeding. So now this makes even less sense. I should have read up on how these pills actually work. I've forgotten. I've been taking them so long that I don't think about it anymore."

"We should have just paid the $50 and gotten your prescription when you were supposed to have it," said Desmond.

"Or pulled out," I said. "Or used condoms. There's a myriad of other things we should have done, but, too fucking late now."

"But a doctor still has to confirm this, right? Those were just home pregnancy tests. They could be wrong."

"They're supposed to be pretty accurate. But yes, I still have to go to a doctor to have it confirmed anyway. I was planning to make the appointment tomorrow."

Desmond put his head in his hands and took a deep breath.

"OK. I need to process this," he said. "I'm going to go for a walk or a drive, or a drink. Something. Is there anything you need from me right now?"

"I don't think so," I said. "I'm good. I mean, I'm not good. I'm freaking the fuck out. But I don't need anything."

"All right. I'll be back later," Desmond said. He kissed me goodbye.

I went to bed early. I couldn't wait to crawl under my covers.

Desmond got home sometime after I'd already been asleep. I was awakened by the sounds of him undressing. The smell of alcohol came off him faintly when he lay down. I opened my eyes to look at him and found him looking back at me. He gently brushed my hair away from my face and kissed my lips. We continued kissing slowly and tenderly for a while. Then he pulled me into him, and I fell asleep against his chest, his chin resting on my head.

I got an appointment for later that week. I took one in the afternoon because there weren't any times available when Desmond would be out of work. I didn't think going to the initial appointment alone would be a big deal anyway. We decided we'd take the situation one step at a time, so we weren't going to discuss it again until after I saw the doctor.

As I suspected, there wasn't much to the appointment. A nurse came into the exam room and asked me what the date of my last period was. I couldn't remember exactly, so I gave my best guess. Then she told to go to the bathroom and pee in the plastic cup she'd left there. About five minutes after I deposited the cup, the nurse came back to my exam room and said I was pregnant. She handed me a little slip of paper with a date on it, circled in blue pen.

"This is your approximate due date," she said with a smile. "June 23rd. You can exit the office to the left."

I stared at the slip of paper all the way out of the clinic to my car. The letters and numerals became peculiar symbols I didn't recognize, like an ancient or futuristic script. Maybe this is just a very vivid dream and I'll wake up in a moment now that I'm aware I'm dreaming, I told myself, but when a moment passed, my surroundings remained intact. My heart first sank, and in another second, it shot up into my throat.

This can't be! I screamed in my head. No! No, no, no, no no! NOOOOO! Maybe it will never really happen—yeah. My stomach will never grow, I'll never go into labor, and I will not end up in a hospital on June 23rd. It's all a bunch of bullshit.

No—Dani, come ON—this is SERIOUS! It's all going happen whether you want it to or not. Oh nooo … No, no, no, no, no!

"So how'd it go?" Desmond asked when he got home from work. I was doing a school assignment in the dining room.

"It's confirmed. I'm pregnant," I said gravely.

To my surprise, there was a hint of a smile on Desmond's face. He looked to the floor in a way that felt suspicious of trying to fight back a full toothy grin.

Then, he came to me and took my hands into his.

"Come sit with me for a few minutes," he said. "I want to talk." I said all right, and he led me, still holding my hands, to the couch. He sat me down, but he remained standing.

"I've been doing a lot of thinking," he said. He starting pacing as he spoke, from one end of the couch to the wall. "We've been together for years. *I love you.* I can't see my future with anyone but you. So maybe this baby isn't such a bad thing. I wanted this to happen eventually. It's earlier than I planned for sure, but I think we can make it work. I mean, I've got a decent job, and you know Bobby's been paying me to do sound for him at The Rubber Mill. He asked me to record his next album too, and he'll be paying me for that as well, so I figure I can keep taking on recording projects to make extra money. Maybe one day that will be my main source of income and I won't need the construction job anymore. But that's neither here nor there. Once you finish school, you're going to get a nice job, so then we should be set. If, god forbid, we were really struggling, I know my mom would let us live with them for a while. She'd convince my dad if he didn't want us to. Once that kid comes into the world, you won't be able to keep her from them. I bet my mom would even watch them for us while we're at work so we don't have to pay for childcare. She loves kids. She really wanted more kids but couldn't have them after her accident. "

"So you're totally on board with having a baby …"

"Yes. The other thing I'm trying to say—the main point that I was coming to—is that I want to do this right. I want to marry you."

"Like, now?" I said.

"Or after the baby is born. Whenever you prefer. But I want to be engaged for real. I don't want this to be one of those situations where we say, yeah, we're getting married eventually, and we just keep putting it off. I'm serious about this. I want to get you a ring and set a date, make it official. You deserve that. I know you've always dreamed of getting married."

"Wait, so, are you proposing?"

"Well, I want to do that the right way too—like, buy the ring first and get down on one knee. I'm just letting you know that I'm ready to do it. I'm ready to take care of you and do what I have to do to make this work with us and the baby."

"Do you have money for a ring?"

"I've been putting away some of my side project money, so I have a little something. It might not be the most expensive ring or have the biggest rock in it, but you'll have one," he said with a laugh.

"I really don't care how fancy it is," I said. I was beginning to feel flushed. I rubbed my sweaty palms on my thighs and breathed deeply.

"You don't seem happy," said Desmond.

"I'm just a little overwhelmed."

Desmond stood back, appearing a bit offended. Then his expression mellowed and he said, tilting my chin up softly with his thumb and index finger, "That's OK. These are all big decisions to be made. We don't have to figure it all out right now."

"Um, hello? The timer is ticking," I said, looking down at my stomach.

"I'm not saying let's take nine months. I mean, like, a week or two. Just take *a little* time to think over everything we talked about, get your head right." said Desmond.

TWENTY

I did practically nothing but think it over. I walked around like all my brains had fallen out of my head except the part that was thinking it over. I forgot where I was heading on campus, what people said to me the instant they said it. I was nearly getting into car accidents. How will I tell my family? I wondered. When will I want to get married? Should we move, or should we stay in the same house? What will it be like trying to get through my last semester of school, possibly the most rigorous one of my college career, plus working, during my third trimester? When can I realistically start my first real job with a newborn? Will I still be able to play in a band when I become a mom? Will I have time to do anything I want to do anymore?

It seemed my mother never got to be her own person when we were young. When she wasn't at work, she was doing work at home—cleaning up after us, helping us with homework, paying bills, making sure everything that needed to be handled for our health and education was handled, usually neglecting her own in the process. The only thing she did that you could call a hobby was gardening, and she may have done it more to keep the neighbors from gossiping about her poor yard maintenance than for enjoyment. I should have been more helpful around the house as a child.

Ardis Alchemy had a mini trip scheduled the next week. Thursday night, we were playing a show in Detroit. Friday, we were playing in Ann Arbor. Saturday and Sunday were shows in Chicago. We took Gabby's SUV, which we were able to fit ourselves and all our equipment in by removing most of the seats.

Gabby had an old friend who lived in Ann Arbor, so we went straight to her place after our show in Detroit and stayed until Saturday morning. In Chicago, we stayed with a friend of Mina, our third bassist. Most of her musical experience was in classical guitar, but all her practice in the fingerstyle made bass an easy transition for her.

Normally, I'd be jittery before going on stage. The jitters would go away once we got into our first song. This time, my nerves were too shocked to be felt. I was calmly numb, sedated-like.

I knew I couldn't drink anymore but that avoiding alcohol without anyone asking questions would be tricky business since there'd likely be drinking everywhere we went, and I really didn't want to explain myself. When Gabby's friend had a small get together Friday night and offered us beer and wine, I said I felt really dehydrated and just wanted some water.

On our way to Chicago, Gabby mentioned that Cameron wanted to come watch us.

"Do you guys mind?" she asked.

"Of course not," Mina responded instantaneously. She was sitting in the one seat we'd left in the back. I was in the passenger seat. Gabby glanced over at me for an answer.

"No," I said, even though I actually did mind, because I knew what was to be expected with Cameron: drama. I wasn't about to tell her she couldn't bring her boyfriend around though when I, myself, had a boyfriend who people in my life simply tolerated, and Desmond had crashed some of Gabby's house parties, so that made it seem even more unfair to object to Cameron's presence.

Cameron arrived at our last show with Nick. On Cameron's shirt was a button reading, "Ask Me!" with an arrow pointing toward a Purple Heart that was pinned on beside it.

After our set, we reloaded the car and then went back inside to find a table for the five of us so that we could watch the rest of the bands.

Cameron said, "I want to buy you ladies a round to congratulate you on all your gigs. It's so exciting that you're playing in different cities."

Gabby and Mina gave him their drink orders.

"What will you have, Dani?" he asked.

"I'm not drinking tonight," I said.

"Why not?" asked Gabby.

"I'm trying to control my weight better. Thought I should cut down my alcohol intake."

"You look fine," Gabby said, giving me a light shove on the shoulder.

"If you change your mind Dani, I'm still good for it," said Cameron.

After he brought back their drinks, Mina said to him, "So I'm asking … What's with the medal on your shirt?"

"Some guy—total stranger—was sitting next to me in a bar in Cleveland, and he said, 'Here—I want you to have this.' I was like, 'Man, I can't take that!' And he was like, 'No, please. Please take it. I don't want it anymore. I need you to have this.' I didn't want to keep arguing with him, so I took it."

"Seriously? Just like that?" Mina said.

"Yeah—seriously!" Cameron replied.

"Why are you wearing it though?" I asked him, not trying to curb the criticism in my voice even the slightest. "I don't think it's meant to be worn on a t-shirt like that."

"Nah, I think it should be displayed proudly like so. And the color really brings out my eyes," he said, batting his eye lashes.

Suddenly, a server brought a beer to me. "This is from the gentleman over there," she said, nodding at a table that was three away from ours where a group of guys were sitting. I looked over, and one of the guys locked eyes with me and smiled. I recognized him from the crowd during our set.

"Oooh, you have an admirer!" said Mina.

Gabby gave me a jab in the side with her elbow and said, "You *have* to drink that one."

"Right." I answered.

I went the bathroom, bringing my beer along, and poured most of it into the toilet so that it would appear

I'd been drinking it. Once they were all a couple rounds in, I stealthily placed my unfinished glass with their collection of empty ones at the end of the table to be taken away by an employee.

Near the end of the last band's timeslot, Cameron and Nick said they were going outside for a minute. The bouncer stopped them as they were trying to exit the front door. We were sitting close enough to witness their conversation.

"Hey, what's that on your shirt?" the bouncer said. Cameron told him the same story he told us.

"I think you better give that back to whoever you got it from," said the bouncer, his face stern.

"He wanted me to keep it, so I'm keeping it," said Cameron with a shrug, and he and Nick pushed past him.

"Gabby," I said, "if you want your boyfriend to survive the end of the night, I think you better tell him to take off the Purple Heart. I'm pretty sure the bouncer is going to beat the living shit out of him if he walks back in here wearing that thing."

"I know. He didn't even really get it from a guy at a bar. He bought it at a pawn shop. He thought it was cool."

"What? What would possess someone to make up a story like that?" I said.

"I have no idea," Gabby said with a sigh. "I'll talk to him though."

When Cameron and Nick came back, Nick was carrying a guitar case. Gabby pulled Cameron aside to talk to him. After they were done, he removed the Purple Heart and button from his shirt.

Nick and Cameron walked onto the stage once the band finished breaking down their equipment. Oh, *that's why* Cameron wanted to come to this show, I thought to myself. He and Nick had been doing this Flight of the Conchords sort of thing where they'd play silly songs, but they'd ask the audience to give them the topics for the songs and write them on the spot. Nick played guitar and Cameron came up with the lyrics and sang.

Nick opened the guitar case and pulled out my shiny, transparent purple burst Ibanez RG. Apparently, that's what he and Cameron had gone outside for. I hadn't even realized it was *my* case in his hand.

I hurried to the stage and said to Nick, "What are you doing with my guitar?"

He now had one of my cables plugged into the guitar's input jack and was going to connect it to the club's amp sitting on the stage.

"Cam said that you said I could borrow it."

"I meant to tell you, Dani—Nick broke the G string on his guitar a little bit ago, and he didn't bring any extras, and, as you know, that's a pretty important string, so we really need your guitar. I promise he'll return it in the same condition it's in now or I'll replace it, and you can punch me. Scout's honor," said Cameron, giving me the three-finger scout hand sign.

"Fine," I said, and I went back to our table.

Cameron started their set with his usual introduction.

"Hey. How's it going? I'm Cameron, and this is Nick. We're going to play some songs for you ladies and gents, but you get to tell us what they're about. So what I need is for you to throw out some song topic ideas. Just shout 'em out. Go ahead."

"Big butts," one guy yelled.

His buddy next to him chimed in, "Big tits."

A girl at the next table said, "Big dicks!" and high-fived her giggling friend while shooting a smug look at the two guys.

"Well, that's three topics," said Cameron, "but that's all right. I think we can work with this. Big butts, big tits, big dicks. Here we go. A one, two, one, two, three."

Nick played a couple bars alone, and then Cameron started:

Some guys want a girl
With big tits
And other guys
They want big asses
When a female comes around
All well-endowed
These types of dudes
Start making passes
And a lot of ladies
They will say
That these guys are pricks
So they go to the gay clubs
And dance with men
Who like
Really big dicks.

By this point, the bouncer had crept up to the stage. He was staring fiercely at Cameron, but Cameron kept going.

If you ask me
What I'm into
I will tell you
Just look at my girlfriend
She really has it all
Such smarts and class
And it doesn't hurt
She's also got
Big tits
And a big ass

Yes she does
Oh yeah she does
Yes she do
And Nick does too.

Gabby gasped when Cameron started singing about her, and her eyes bugged out in surprise. Then, she laughed and shook her head.

"He's wild, isn't he?" she said to me.

"He's something all right," I answered.

The audience's responses at the end of the song were a mixed bag of cheers, blank faces, and boos.

When they started their second song about farting, the sound guy cut the mic, and the bouncer yanked Cameron away from it by the arm.

"You weren't scheduled for a set. This ain't a free-for-all. Show's over," said the bouncer. His voice rang out in the quieted room.

He escorted Cameron all the way to the door as Nick packed my gear. Since the bouncer wouldn't let

Cameron and Nick have re-entrance and told them to never come back, we decided it was a good time for us all to head home.

After class on Monday, Gabby asked if I wanted to get food or drinks. I told her food was fine and to meet me at a nearby cafe.

"So you're still intent on not drinking I take it?" she said.

"Yeah," I said, looking down into my lap. I didn't like being reminded of my secret. It was becoming too exhausting. *But this is Gabby.* Maybe she can know it.

I leaned in closer to her, and in a low voice, I told her, "I didn't want to say anything around Mina or the other people we were hanging out with over the weekend, so please, don't repeat this: I'm pregnant."

"Oh. That's why ..." I could see she was quite surprised, but it was indeterminable to me whether her personal feelings regarding the news were positive or negative, and I was kind of glad about it. "So what are you going to do?"

"I'm not sure yet," I said. "Desmond seems to want to keep it. He's talking about getting married."

"Whoa—girl!" she leaned across the table and squeezed my arm. "That's huge!"

"I guess so," I said.

She sat back and examined my face.

"Is that not what you want?" she asked.

"I really don't know, Gabby. I'm confused at the moment."

"Hmm." Gabby pressed her lips together tightly and nodded her head understandingly.

"I have a confession to make," she said. "I was pregnant once too."

"By Cameron?!" I said.

"Yes. It was eight months ago that I found out. I miscarried before I actually knew. I was having this terrible cramping and heavy bleeding. It scared me, because I never have periods like that, and I wasn't expecting a period, so I went to the campus clinic. The nurse practitioner told me it was a miscarriage."

"Did you tell Cameron?"

"After I left the clinic, I walked around downtown by myself just crying. I probably looked like a crazy woman. I didn't make eye contact with anyone. I was staring right through everything—like, just so lost in my head, you know? I almost got hit by a bus. I went to Cameron's that night, and that's when I told him. He was really sweet about it. He held me all night in his bed."

"Would you have kept it if you hadn't miscarried?" I asked her.

"Maybe. It's hard to say. It didn't feel real since it was over so fast." Gabby squeezed my arm again, her eyes soft with sympathy. "Just know that I'm here for you, whatever you need."

TWENTY-ONE

The next evening, Ron told Desmond he had "some really good weed" he wanted to smoke with him, so we went to the Carveys' house.

I followed Mandy to the kitchen to make some tea.

"How are you feeling?" she asked, this shine in her eyes. Does she know, I wondered? Nah ... How could she?

"I'm feeling fine," I said.

"*Good*! So, how about an herbal tea? Let's see—I have peppermint leaf. That can help relieve nausea. Lemon balm—that's another good option for you."

She does know! Mandy fancied herself to have a touch of clairvoyance. This had me believing it too.

"Peppermint leaf works for me."

We took our tea into the living room, where Ron was telling Desmond how some guy he worked with had hooked up with an elderly woman they completed an HVAC job for. This compelled Ron to bring up another story about when he *almost* had sex with a much older woman—his uncle's girlfriend. Ron was eight years old, and his uncle was babysitting him. He thought it would be funny if his girlfriend took Ron's virginity. After his uncle did a lot of arm twisting and waving his pistol around, his girlfriend finally agreed. Ron said he locked himself in the bathroom and was able escape through the window before she could get to him. He ran away to his grandma's house, and his uncle was never allowed to watch him again—not that Ron's parents did a much better job of it. His step-dad would punch him, and his mom would sometimes burn him with cigarettes and punish him by not feeding him, so he'd steal food from the store and kids at school.

Ron sank back into the couch and stretched his arms and legs. "Anyway, nothing's really new around here. Our refrigerator broke again last week, that piece of shit. I told your mom this is the last time I try to fix it. If it breaks again, we're getting a new one. Seeing Chuck seduce that old broad a few days ago is the most interesting thing that's gone on with me recently." He chortled.

"Wow. What a boring life you must have then," Desmond said.

"Hey, pretty soon, this is gonna be your life, buddy. I can see it now—you and Dani are gonna be just like me and your mom, hanging out in your house that you're sick of, shit breaking all the time, on a street you're sick of too. We can't sell this fuckin' place right now, unfortunately. And you know, you're lookin' more like me every day. Why don't you lean in a little closer? I'll knock that front tooth out and make you a spitting image," said Ron.

"I'm not gonna make it that easy for you," said Desmond, cracking a crooked smile.

On the drive home, I told Desmond that I thought Mandy knew I was pregnant.

"Yeah … I meant to talk to you about that. I told her," he said.

"What?! Desmond! Why would you do that?"

"Stressed. Excited." He shrugged. "She won't tell anybody. Trust me. She had to learn to be a good secret keeper so my dad wouldn't be losing his shit all the time over the stupid stuff my brothers and I did."

"Well, I guess I should confess that I told Gabby," I said. "It was getting too hard to hide from her."

"What did she say?" asked Desmond.

"Nothing really."

The next day, Lee and I took our walk in a part of the Tremont neighborhood that's uphill from one of the steel mills. I liked going to this vantage point on the hill to see the torch-like flame of the steel mill's blast furnace, which burns dependably at all hours, next to the city's skyline. The sky had begun to get dark by early evening, so the furnace flame and downtown lights were already in their most luminous states when we arrived.

As I took in the view, the words "pretty soon, this is gonna be your life" kept echoing inside me. They felt like a group of bullies ganging up on me, coming to force my head in the toilet and flush until the dreams in it were all flushed away.

If Desmond freaks out over a dropped plate, what will he do when a kid colors on the wall or breaks a window with a baseball, or when a bigger and more serious problem comes our way, I wondered? There's no telling anymore what he's capable of. And I can't just disappear with the baby. Desmond or his family will go to the police. I'd need proof that he hurt us or put us in danger to take to the police, and by then, it may be too late for the baby or me. I don't want to deal with all these potential legal messes anyway. I can't stand the thought of the kind of father Desmond might be, or the thought of having a child who could grow up to be like him.

After we'd left the hill and gone back to the neighborhood streets, the wind picked up. I watched a scattering of leaves frantically scrape down the pavement on their crispy, curled-up edges, looking like a swarm of people running from a tidal wave, and I felt an urgency to make moves on a decision. Survival instinct kicked in. You will not be dragged along into these circumstances, I told myself. You're going to find the courage to tell Desmond no, to everything. Tonight.

Later at home, I sat next to Desmond on the couch, a notebook and a piece of paper inscribed with a writing assignment in my lap. He was watching TV. I pretended to brainstorm a response for the assignment so I could prep for the conversation.

"Desmond," I said, putting my pen down thoughtfully like I was pulling myself out of some really intense focusing. "I've done a lot of thinking, and, I really don't want to have a baby or get married right now. The time isn't right. I want to have an abortion."

Desmond closed his eyes for a moment and sighed.

"OK," he said, pushing his hair back with his fingers. "I kind of figured, but I was hoping ..."

He took his bong off the coffee table and packed it. I returned to my fake working while he smoked.

"So what now?" he asked when he was done.

"I have to make an appointment at a clinic that performs abortions," I said. "Health insurance might cover the procedure, but the thing is, I'm still on my dad's policy, and I don't want this brought up to my parents, because they'll probably tell the rest of my family. I think we should pay for it out-of-pocket. I was wondering, since you're not going to … um … need money for a ring now … if you wouldn't mind footing the bill, and then I'll pay my half of it back as soon as I can." I couldn't bring myself to look at him while I was speaking. I stared straight ahead at the TV screen, my voice becoming lower and frailer the closer I got to the part where I had to ask him about paying.

"Fuck, Dani," he groaned.

"You'll get the money back ASAP. I swear! I'll sell some of my music gear if I have to."

"I guess I really have no other option, so, fine," he said.

"Thank you. I promise I'll pay you back," I said, placing my hand on his shoulder.

"All right. I get it—you'll pay me back," he said, sounding annoyed. He slipped his shoulder away from my touch. Then, a moment later, he pulled me in for a long, tight hug.

I wondered how Desmond would tell Mandy. I felt broken hearted and ill with guilt at the idea of her disappointment.

I was terrified to see my own family react to the situation since abortion is against Catholic belief—

hence why I decided it best that they never found out about it. The Church is also against birth control, but I always knew that, at least, didn't matter to my family. Pretty much all Catholics ignore the contraception ban. It's just one of a handful of Church bans many casually disregard due to their acceptance of modern social norms. I couldn't be another of these cafeteria Catholics though; it didn't seem right. So, I'd started considering myself a lapsed Catholic.

On the occasions that my parents imposed Mass upon me, such as Christmas Eve Mass, which we traditionally attended as a family before heading to the Carminos' annual Christmas Eve party, or Mass on Mother's Day, preceding our usual brunch with the Moran side in the party room of a restaurant near Holy Rosary, I felt like an imposter, especially while receiving the Eucharist. It's too bad, I'd think as I sat there in the pew, how lovely I still find Catholic churches to look at with all their stained glass and elaborately-painted ceilings and glittering gold altars, and how the sad but hopeful melodies they play during services, like the vibrations of a lone soul traveling the high seas, onward to a new life, still give me chills.

I used to have this patron saint charm bracelet. Each oval charm resembled a fresco of a saint. It was so colorful and vintage-looking, like a necklace I also owned, which had a round pendant displaying a baby-blue-clad Virgin Mary with red roses at her feet. Wearing those pieces of jewelry began to feel hypocritical and irreverent, and I hated it, because I loved them.

I'd miss all these little pieces of the religious life I lived so authentically as a child, the way you might miss little things about an ex when you're reminded of them like their smell or sense of humor without missing the relationship itself because you know it's not the right one for you anymore.

I wondered if my family would stop inviting me over for Christmas and Easter if they knew I referred to myself as a lapsed Catholic. I pictured my mom saying, "Since Dani doesn't believe anymore, she really has no business celebrating either holiday with us."

It could be even worse than them disinviting me to holiday parties. They could disown me. Well, maybe the *whole* family won't disown me. My brothers most likely don't care about my faith, and I don't think some of my cousins do either, so I'll still have them.

Perhaps it would be more permissible to my church-going relatives if I converted to another religion rather than ceasing the practice of it altogether, because at least I'd still have God in my life. I was always hearing how much better things are when you have God in your life. When kids act up in school, it's because their parents didn't put God in their life, Grandpa Jack, my father's father, would say. There might be some truth to that; maybe we all just need something to believe in order to lift ourselves up.

I could convert to a faith that's pro-choice, like Reform Judaism. Grandma Celia had once said to me that the Cleveland Jewish community has always had a friendly relationship with the Cleveland Catholic community, so she may not mind my conversion, and then nobody else would either, and I wouldn't be excommunicated, and I might even be welcomed over for the major Catholic holidays. Even if I'm not really taken with any new religion but use it as a front to keep peace with the family, who has to know?

But maybe my family isn't as close and wonderful as I thought if I have to go to such measures to prevent them from kicking me out of it. Maybe my idea of them is just another giant illusion.

TWENTY-TWO

I took the first available appointment at the clinic, which was on a Monday. Because Desmond's job was inflexible and gave very limited time off, he told me he couldn't come with me on a weekday. He signed a check for me to bring and fill in with the cost of the visit when I knew what it would be, and I asked Gabby to come with me instead. She agreed. I met her at her dorm and she drove us in case I was sedated and not in the condition to drive afterward.

A group of anti-choice protesters were demonstrating in the space of blacktop between the parking lot and the building when we arrived. I read one of their signs. "Woman up! Accept consequences or burn in hell!" it said.

So I guess they disregard a costly medical procedure and the stigmatization for having it as consequences, I thought.

I remembered that in fifth grade, we were assigned to design a pro-life poster for Theology. The posters were to be entered in a diocesan-wide competition for school children, and the winning one would be displayed at a Right to Life rally.

I knew nothing about abortion. It wasn't discussed in school until eighth grade Sex Ed. All I knew was I wanted to win what was, in my eyes, an art contest.

My poster received an honorable mention. My teacher hung it up on the "Best Work Wall" in the hallway, where A-plus work and other exceptionally-done assignments got to go. I drew a mother holding her baby beside the father, who had one hand on the mother's shoulder and the other over the baby's bundled-up little body, and both the mother and father were smiling. As if a loving, happy family is the destiny awaiting every fetus carried to term ... I was particularly proud of how the faces and hands turned out. I'd been trying to master human features since second grade.

Right through the glass doors of the clinic was a waiting room. I went up to the counter to sign in, and a staff member behind the window handed me a stack of forms to fill out. When I returned with the forms, the woman at the window gave them the customary once over, then sat down at the computer and said, "OK, I'll get you entered into our system. And when would you like to schedule your next appointment? I can also set that up for you now."

"Next appointment?" I said. "I'm sorry, what appointment are you speaking of?"

The woman gently answered, "State law mandates a 24-hour wait period after counseling to think on your decision before you can have the procedure. An ultrasound is also required, so all we'll be doing today is the ultrasound and counseling."

"Are you serious?" I said. Like I would just show up without putting any thought at all into what I was about to do. "I missed school for this! I made my friend come all the way out here! This is a time-sensitive matter! Why did no one explain this on the phone?!"

"I'm very sorry for the miscommunication and any inconvenience," the woman said, sounding smaller and shrinking back a bit.

I stomped back to my chair, seeing spots from my fury, and told Gabby what was going on.

"That's so fucking stupid. I'm really sorry, Dani," said Gabby. "I guess just schedule whenever works for you and I'll try my best to be here again."

I marched back up to the window and waited until I got the attention of the woman who had been helping me before. I sensed that I'd caused some uneasiness among the rest of the staff squeezed into the tight confines of the administrative area.

"I'd like to schedule my next appointment," I said to her, attempting to appear collected despite still being enraged. She was able to fit me in on Thursday.

I was first taken back into an exam room for the ultrasound. It was performed by a male doctor named Dr. Connor.

"There's one heartbeat," he said to me. "You're about nine weeks along. Would you like to see the image?"

"Sure," I said.

I was merely curious. Looking at it, I didn't feel any different. It was like seeing a picture in a textbook or one of those plastic anatomical models in a classroom.

After that, I was escorted by a staff member to a small space that reminded me of an interrogation room with a rectangular, wooden table and two chairs. I was told to have a seat and wait for the doctor. Dr. Connor had told me he'd also be handling my counseling.

When he came in, Dr. Connor sat down across from me at the table with his clipboard in front of him and got right down to explaining how the abortion would go.

"So we'll be doing suction," he said. "A sedative and local anesthetic are available for pain and cramping. Just make sure to have someone with you who can drive you home."

"My friend is going to drive me," I said.

"OK, good. So basically, we open the cervix, and then we insert a tube that's attached to the machine that does the suction. It's very safe, and it'll be over in minutes. Any questions?"

I shook my head.

"All right. Now, I can also get you started on birth control. Would you like to give me a pharmacy to use?"

"I'm already on birth control," I said.

"Very good," said Dr. Connor. "Next, I need you to read this script from the state."

He freed a white legal paper from his clipboard and handed it to me. He was silent as I skimmed over the document, which included some content about fetal development, referring to the fetus as "an independent human life," though Ohio law only allowed abortion up to 20 weeks post-fertilization, a timeframe in which a fetus is still considered inviable, meaning incapable of surviving outside the womb even with a ventilator due to lack of development, or, in other words, dependent.

Seeing that I was done reading the script, Dr. Connor removed more materials from his clipboard and said, "OK, so, if you were to decide to continue the pregnancy, there's a booklet here that talks about your options and available support, and there's another with more details on the stages of fetal development." He held them out to me.

"I really don't need them. You can just keep them and save some paper," I said.

"I'm required to give these to you," he said. "You can do with them what you want. I also have to inform you that if you were to continue the pregnancy, the man involved in it would be obligated to pay child support. Other responsibilities he would have are noted in the first booklet I mentioned. Is there anything you'd like to ask?"

"Nope."

"Well then we're done for today. I'll see you when you come back. Take care," said Dr. Connor. He stood up from the table to leave and smiled at me—a closed-mouth, tight-lip smile. I didn't get up to leave until he closed the door behind him. I tossed the materials he gave me in a recycle bin near the exit to the waiting room.

When Gabby and I walked out of the clinic, I made the mistake of looking in the direction of the protesters again, and one of them, a young woman likely close to our age carrying an "Abortion Is Murder" sign, approached us.

"Miss, did you know that an unborn baby might be able to experience pain by 20 weeks?"

"Oh? Really?" I said sarcastically. I saw Gabby's eyes pop in my peripheral view. "Even if that *might be* true, do they have any awareness? Tell me, what do you remember from when you were a fetus?"

She didn't answer me, so I said to her sharply, "That's what I thought."

Then, in a solemner tone, the young woman said, "The life of an unborn child matters."

"And what about my life?" I shouted, once again enraged. "I guess because I'm no longer a child, mine doesn't matter. The only purpose I serve now is to make another child. What about all the other women in there? Having a baby could cost some of them their lives. It's funny how much someone's life depreciates to people like you as they grow up. Or is it after we've had sex that we become worthless?"

"Dani ..." Gabby murmured behind me. I felt her pull lightly on the edge of my shirt, but I couldn't be stopped in the heat of the moment. I stepped in closer to the protestor, glaring.

"If you don't agree with abortion, just don't ever get one! Exercising my legal right to have one doesn't impede your right not to or your beliefs about it, so why don't you stop trying to step all over other people's rights and beliefs? Take your nasty sign and get the fuck out of my face."

I continued to defiantly glare into the eyes of the young woman, narrowing mine more intensely until she stood down and returned to her clique of circling squawkers, who'd been staring in our direction, their faces confused and nervous.

"Hopefully that'll teach them not to prey on patients," I said to Gabby.

"Are you OK?" she asked. She looked overwhelmed—even a little frightened.

"Yes. I am. I know it probably doesn't seem that way. I'm just angry at this whole situation. Today isn't what I expected. I thought I'd be able to put all this behind me when I walked out of here, but that's not the case. I really appreciate you being here. I'm sorry for the trouble."

"What are friends for?" said Gabby. She smiled and rubbed my shoulder. "Let's get out of here now. I think you've had enough of this place for one day."

"Agreed," I said.

After I got in my car, I texted Desmond to let him know what happened at the clinic and decided I'd visit my café in Berea. I wasn't in the mood to be with anyone or go home, and I'd already planned on skipping class.

Inside the café were the usual college kids, probably from the university nearby. I ordered a cappuccino and sat with it at a small, round table for two near the back entrance, because nobody else was sitting in the back half of the place. I rested my feet on the opposite chair and stared outside at the people coming to and from the shopping plaza across the way.

I thought about how different everything would be if I'd miscarried, feeling a little bitter about it. Instead of accusing me of murder, the likes of the protestors at the clinic would assure me, "God works in mysterious ways. It wasn't meant to be." They'd feel sorry for me. No one would make a fuss about the humanity of the clot-like tissue that fell out of my body or question it being flushed down the toilet rather than given a proper burial.

Then, I pondered the existence of God—something I hadn't felt a need to do in quite some time—and if He had given women inherent control over bringing people into the world, or not bringing them into the world, for a balance of power between us and men and for a means of protection, since, in general, men have the capacity for greater strength, speed, and endurance than women, and if God made the unborn incapable of remembering so that their souls can return to Heaven peacefully if miscarried or aborted and be given new chances of life as other people, or if maybe we don't have souls during fetal development; we're all empty vessels until we emerge into the world. Who can actually prove it's not true? We can't know anything about God's intentions for certain.

But what if abortion is in fact a sin in God's eyes? I imagine He forgives people who must take another's life in war to defeat a greater evil, or for self-defense, or who do it by some tragic accident, so why not someone in my situation too?

Or perhaps the God I'm really dealing with isn't the fashionable compassionate God, but rather, the short-tempered punisher from the Old Testament—a characterization I'd long ago chalked up to ancient political propaganda—and I will feel His wrath for this. So be it I guess.

I was in the dining room listening to *Parallel Lines* in my ear buds while apathetically doing an assignment, Lee lying beside my chair, when Desmond came home.

He put his keys, wallet, and phone on the table without a word and sighed heavily, running his fingers through his hair and pushing it back.

I took my ear buds out.

"Hey. How was your day?" I asked. I could tell his day hadn't been good. I was just trying to initiate communication.

"Sucked," said Desmond, now stretching his arms over his head. He pulled out one of the other chairs, sat down, and yawned.

"Want to talk about it?" I asked.

"Not really," he said. "My boss was being a dick, but that's his usual. Same shit, different day."

"Oh. My day sucked too, as you probably guessed. I was so mad that I had to schedule another appointment, and then I got into it with this protestor outside. I mean, she had it coming. She came up to me. I wasn't looking for a confrontation. I was going to completely ignore them all."

Desmond fluttered his eyelids in disregard. "So what was the appointment actually for then?" he said.

"I had to have an ultrasound, and the doctor talked to me about how the abortion would work. He gave me some reading materials too—stuff about fetal development and my other options in case I were to change my mind."

"Did you see anything during the ultrasound?" he asked.

"Yeah. The doctor asked if I wanted to see the image, and I said 'sure.' I was just curious."

Desmond was quiet. He stared off into the space between himself and table top.

"Shoot, you know what? I forgot to take the check out of my wallet," I said. "I hate carrying a check or a lot of cash around with me. My mom always warned me that if I did, it might get lost or stolen, so I worry."

"It's a reasonable concern," Desmond said dully, still staring off at nothing.

"I'll put it under the change jar," I said. We kept a change jar in one of the kitchen drawers.

So I put the check away, and when I came back to my homework, Desmond looked up at me. Fire had kindled in his eyes.

"You're going to leave, aren't you?" he said.

"What?" I said.

"That's why you want the abortion. It'll give you an easier way out. Once it's paid for, you won't need me anymore. You're going to leave."

"When have I ever said that?"

"You didn't need to. I can tell."

"Well, you're wrong," I said, praying things wouldn't escalate.

Because of the chaos that ensued every time I attempted to leave in the past, even if not permanently, but just to cool off, I was afraid to anymore. It seemed easier to stay and deal with Desmond's mood swings than face the repercussions of making a run for it. And I guess I still had love for him deep down, for reasons I didn't understand, and I was scared to have to rebuild my life by myself, to do things on my own that I'd always had Desmond to help me with. I think I always knew it wasn't right to hang on out of fear and that it wasn't truly what I wanted to do, but I was living in survival mode, just trying to get through each day.

That alone was a hard thing for me to do then, being ground down so far mentally and spiritually. Leaving was a long-term plan at most. Once in a while, I'd whisper to myself, "Someday."

Desmond exploded from his chair and went swiftly to the kitchen.

"Maybe ..." he said beneath the sound of rummaging as I went after him, having a hunch about what he was doing. He slammed shut the drawer where I'd put the check. Then I saw it in his hand. My hunch had been right.

"Maybe I'll just rip up this check and see how simple it is for you to walk away then," he said, holding the check with both hands above his head, one side of it turned down between his thumb and index finger like he was getting ready to tear it.

"Desmond, please, don't! I'm begging you," I said.

"Oh, I'll do it. And you'll have to have the kid after all. Once it comes out, I might just decide to leave *you* and let you take care of it on your own. How's that for a way out?"

"Why would you say that? Desmond, please, we had an agreement." I reached up for the check still being held hostage above Desmond's head in an attempt to snag it, but my short arms were no match for his. He ran back to the dining room, and I went after him. I was so desperate that I fell to my knees.

"Desmond, I swear to you, I'm not going to leave. Please don't rip it up. You gave me your word that you'd help me," I said, my debasement making my lower lip quiver.

"Fine, but this is the only part I'll help you with," said Desmond. "I wouldn't come with you to your doctor appointment even if I could."

He flicked the check into the air, and it fell like a feather to my hands. I put it in my back pocket and later placed it in one of my boots in the corner of the closet.

Desmond then picked up my phone, which was still sitting on the dining room table next to my textbook and laptop with my earbuds plugged into it.

"What are you doing?" I said. "Give it back!"

He yanked the earbuds out as he ran with my phone to our bedroom, punching in my passcode.

"I think your parents should know about this after all," he said, grinning. I made an effort to pull him to the ground by his shirt, which caused him to struggle a bit with scrolling through my contacts. He managed to tug his shirt away from me, splitting it up the middle in the process. He raised the phone above his head like he had the check, his thumb over the call button, and I could see "Mom" on the screen.

TWENTY-THREE

The ringing started. I jumped onto Desmond's back and put one of my hands over his eyes, then tried smacking the phone away from him with my other. Lee had come to investigate the commotion and got into the mix. Desmond tripped on Lee's paw since he couldn't see him underfoot, and Lee squealed in pain, but it was easier to free my phone while Desmond was regaining his balance. The phone thudded to the hardwood floor and slid across it under my dresser.

My mom had picked up. I could faintly hear her voice, dampened by the dresser's plywood underbelly.

"Hello? Dani? Hello?" she said.

Desmond stood with his hands on his hips, staring in the direction of my mother's voice but not making a move. I supposed he stopped having fun and was giving up.

When it seemed my mom had ended the call, I rushed to pick up my phone. Once I had it, I held it tightly to my chest.

"You pull a stunt like that again and I'll go to the police," I said to Desmond.

"For what? Calling your parents?" He laughed. "That's not a crime."

"No, but hitting me is," I said.

"You have me charged with assault, and I'll say you're lying and take you to court. You've hit me before, don't forget, so I can also say I was just defending myself. You have no evidence anyway, so really, you have no case. I, however, have a case against you. You know I can sue you for restitution for having an abortion when I didn't want you to have one?"

"You wouldn't," I said in disbelief. "You're scum. You're the lowest of the low."

"How about we don't talk to the police then, OK? You call the police, and not only will I make court a living hell for you, but I'll go to your parents' house and personally tell them all about this."

"Whatever. Fine," I said.

After staring at me coldly for a moment, Desmond left the room. When I heard him turn on the shower, I changed the passcode in my phone. From then on at home, I kept it hidden inside a sock underneath all the other ones in my sock drawer unless I needed to text or call someone.

When I went to my second appointment at the abortion clinic, it was storming. I guessed that was why there weren't any protesters outside. Gabby wasn't able to take me because she had an important test at school, but she promised to come straight there afterward to pick me up. She said I could stay the night at her place and that we'd come back for my car in the morning.

I signed in at the same counter I did the last time and handed over the check for the amount owed. Then I was told to go to another waiting room down the hall where I'd sign in again.

After I took a seat in this second waiting area, I scanned the whole place. My gaze was drawn to the only other person I saw alone—a 20-something-year-old woman who looked to be in a heated texting conversation. She blotted her cheeks, wet from tears, with a tissue as she waited for her lap to vibrate with the next message from whoever she was talking to. I watched her reading one. The content appeared to pain her. More tears streamed down her face. They were starting to soak the edge of her white hijab near her cheekbones.

A young couple was sitting across from me. They seemed about my age—maybe even younger. They held hands in silence, occasionally looking into each other's eyes and smiling that way people do when they're trying to get *you* to smile.

There was another woman blotting her face with a tissue as someone who resembled her enough to be her sister patted and stroked her back. I figured they were both middle-aged.

When the door opened again, I compulsively turned my head to see who would walk through it. There was a woman wearing a black pants suit and black heels with a very young girl, probably no older than 11.

They sat at the far end of the row I was in. I fought the urge to turn my head in their direction again. The woman quietly said to the girl, "Would you like me to take you to your aunt's after this, or would you like to stay with me for a while?"

"I don't care," I heard the girl say, her voice flat. I strained my ears to listen to her. "I just don't want to go back to my dad's house."

"You will never have to go there again," the woman said.

"Actually, I want to stay with you for a while," said the girl.

They were the last new people I saw come into the waiting room before I was called. A nurse named Jamie took me back to another interrogation room where I had to watch a short video in which a young woman played a patient preparing to have an abortion. The actor said that around one in four American women have an abortion in their lifetimes and that she was at peace with her decision to go through with the procedure after having thought and prayed hard about it. Once the video ended, Jamie took me to an exam room.

"Do you have someone driving you home?" she asked.

"Yes," I said.

"OK. Are they in the waiting room? I can have them escorted to the recovery area when we're all finished," she said.

"No. She's actually not here right now, but she'll be here to pick me up."

"We're not authorized to give you any kind of sedative or anesthetic if the person driving you home isn't physically present at the time of your appointment. It's a safety policy. We can't risk incapacitated patients trying to drive themselves home. The most I can give you is some ibuprofen. If you want it, I suggest taking it right now."

"All right. I guess I'll take it then," I said.

She gave me one large, white ibuprofen tablet and a paper cup of water to help me get it down. After I swallowed the tablet, she handed me a hospital gown.

"I'm going to leave you to change now," she said. "I'll be back in a few minutes with the doctor."

Before I changed, I texted Gabby to tell her there was no need to come since I'd be able to operate a vehicle.

Jamie was joined by another nurse when she returned with Dr. Connor.

"I'm Sasha," the new nurse said to me, smiling.

Jamie and Sasha helped Dr. Connor set up the machine that would be used. I waited on top of the crunchy, white strip of paper covering the sticky, plastic exam table. Though I was still wearing my socks, my feet were so cold that they hurt, and I could feel goosebumps popping up on my arms and legs.

When they were done prepping, Jamie said to me, "Now, I'm going to ask you to lie back so we can insert dilating rods and get started."

Sasha came to the side of the table and took my hand once we began. "You'll experience some cramping," she said to me. "It feels a little different for everyone. You can squeeze my hand if you'd like."

In a moment, I was having long, deep pangs. It was like a knife was being pushed down into my lower belly. The panging got longer to the point of becoming continuous, as though I'd grown infinite layers of tissue to be sliced through, and I felt dizzy and nauseous.

I picked up my head to get a look at Dr. Connor. I was hoping for some kind of indication that we were almost done. I didn't want to watch the machine working, which it was doing pretty loudly, so I tried to see past it. However, I accidentally got a glimpse of rusty fluid moving through a tube from my peripheral view.

Dr. Connor looked stern, concerned, hyper-focused. I couldn't get a sense of how far along we were.

"Sasha," I croaked, afraid I wasn't going to be able to hold in my vomit as I spoke, "I don't feel well." My body had turned as icy-cold all over as my feet, but I was sweating profusely.

"Her face is gray," Sasha said. Jamie went into a drawer at the washing station and pulled out a blood pressure gauge. She strapped it around my arm and pumped it.

"60 over 40. Shit," Jamie said.

"Oh my goodness," said Sasha. She wiped away a few wet strands of hair that had been clinging to my forehead.

Jamie stood watching me for a moment. There was a flicker of fear in her eyes.

My vision went dark and spotty, and I could barely feel any part of myself but my uterus, where the pain was still cutting through clearly.

I looked to the wall. I focused every shred of my dwindling consciousness into putting coherent sentences together in my mind to maintain control of it.

My name is Dani. I was born in Cleveland. The grass is green. The sky is blue. A dog ran in the park. The dog chased a cat. The cat chased a mouse. The mouse ate some cheese. The woman rode the train into town. She went shopping.

"OK, I think I got it all," I heard Dr. Connor say.

I tried to see his face through my haze. He appeared relieved, but still stern.

She bought a hat. My dog's name is Lee. I'm studying journalism.

The machine was shut off and the tube quickly removed from me. Dr. Connor pushed the machine out of the room, and I was left with Sasha and Jamie.

Jamie brought me another paper cup of water. I tilted my head forward and carefully drank, taking shallow breaths between each sip. I gradually increased the depth of my breaths as the nausea waned and my vision refocused and brightened.

When I felt I was stable enough to stand, Sasha helped me down from the exam table, holding my arm in case I was unbalanced. She brought my clothes to me from the chair in the corner of the room where I'd laid them after I put on the gown. To my surprise, Jamie pulled my shirt over my head, and Sasha held out my underwear and pants for me to step into. I gripped the edge of the table as I did to prevent myself from falling over.

"You don't have to help me put my shoes on," I said to them, though I appreciated their kindness. I sat in the chair so it was easier to wedge my feet through the narrow, stretchless openings of my Chucks.

"Here, you'll need this," said Jamie. She handed me a thick pad. "You'll probably want to put it in your underwear now. We can leave you to it and meet you outside the room to take you to the recovery area, unless you'd like assistance."

"I can do it on my own, but thanks," I said.

In the recovery area, Jamie seated me in a titled-back, faux-leather chair, like the kind in the dentist's office.

"I want you to stay here for a while," she said. "Don't leave until I say you can."

"OK," I said. She walked away momentarily and returned with a granola bar and bottle of water for me.

After I consumed the granola bar and almost all the water, I rested my head against the chair and closed my eyes. The next time I opened them, 45 minutes had passed.

Jamie came back with the blood pressure gauge.

"How are we doing here?" she said.

"I feel good," I told her.

"Let's take your blood pressure again," she said. She reported it was much better after getting a reading. "You're welcome to stay longer, but if you want to go now, I'm comfortable with that."

"All right. I think I'll leave now. Thanks for everything," I said.

"Of course. Take care of yourself." Jamie looked a little apprehensive, but warm.

I walked through the nearest exit and found myself beneath an awning on a side of the building that was out of site from my car. The rain and wind that had been whipping against the brick outer walls when I arrived had ceased. The air hugged me with the sweetness of rain-soaked blacktop. Some of the gray cloud cover had given way to the sun, creating a fluorescent-like glow over the wet world.

A robin poked its head out of bush to the left. I imagined it was checking to see if the storm had passed. It turned its head from side to side, and, apparently pleased by what it saw, hopped out of the soft, flat needles. It took a couple more hops forward, spread its wings, and flew away. I watched it until it disappeared into the clouds. I wondered if it knew exactly where it was heading or was simply roaming. I then got my bearings, located my car, and went home.

TWENTY-FOUR

When Desmond returned from work that evening, I was resting on the couch, watching TV. He said hello. I asked him how his day was. He said it was fine. He never asked about my day, but I couldn't stand the tension, so I started telling him about it.

"I got super sick and faint during the procedure. They made me stay longer after to recover. Because Gabby wasn't there yet when they called me back to the exam room, they wouldn't give me any sedative or anesthetic. I told her not to worry about coming to get me and drove myself home. I was going to spend the night at her dorm originally."

All he said was, "Uh huh," keeping his eyes down on his boots as he loosened the laces and tugged them off his feet.

"I'm going to take it easy the rest of the night and probably go to bed early, just so you know," I said.

"Bobby's coming over to lay tracks, so I'll be in the studio all night anyway," he said. That was that.

The next day after school, Gabby and I discussed everything in more detail, sitting cross-legged on her bed with pizza rolls and tea.

"It sucks that it made you feel so sick, but I'm sure it was still way less difficult and dangerous than giving birth," said Gabby.

"Oh, for sure," I said.

I remembered when Aunt Linda explained to me what childbearing is actually like back in high school. I felt as though she'd revealed the biggest conspiracy that ever existed when I discovered how much gory detail had so casually been left out of Sex Ed.—the vaginal tearing, losing control of your bowels, the afterbirth. Then there's the whole peeing every time you laugh from then on thing and the stretch marks that they never mentioned. And how during the pregnancy, there's the possibility for developing illnesses like diabetes and liver disease. And they don't tell you anything about how to prepare your body for labor or the ways to make it easier for yourself, or that women sometimes still die during labor.

"So remember that when you're with a guy," Aunt Linda said. "Ask yourself if he's worthy of all the work and pain you'll have to go through to bring his child into the world."

As promised, I paid Desmond back for half the medical bill. Afraid to even utter the word "abortion" to him, I just said, "Here's what I owe you." He gave a single nod of recognition, and neither of us ever brought the ordeal up again.

Meghan was working the next time I went to the bar. She said hi to me as soon as she saw me. I asked her how she'd been doing. She told me well and poured me a vodka with Sprite.

"Do you still talk to Riley?" I asked her. That's the girl who wanted braces and glasses and acne.

"I do!" said Meghan. "In fact, we're still pretty good friends. She lives in South Carolina now. Her husband's a Marine, and he was stationed there."

"Oh. That's nice for her," I said.

"Yeah. She seems happy. I also talk to Claire Zajac and Colleen O'Rourke. That's really it from Holy Rosary, but I do see a lot of others from grade school here at the bar. Basically anybody who still lives in the neighborhood. What about you? Do you talk to anyone from Holy Rosary?"

"Bernadette Lipinski," I said.

"That makes sense. I remember you two were inseparable."

"That we were. She's in school in Connecticut now."

"It's nice to have old friends," said Meghan.

The other bartender had been shooting looks at us. "Hey, Meghan," he said, nodding toward a man who'd been sitting drinkless for a couple minutes.

"I better go help him," Meghan said. "Let me know when you need another drink."

Claire and Colleen went to St. Ambrose too, but I'd been good at ignoring them like I had Meghan. I wondered what we'd think of each other if we met again—if we could be cool like Meghan and I were.

Claire and Bernadette had been mortal enemies in grade school, so Claire disliked me by default, and by the same principle, Claire's best friend, Colleen, hated us both. I'm not even sure how the grudge between Bern and Claire came about. It may have been because of this time at a birthday sleepover we all went to in second grade. That's before cliques really form, you know? Parents invite every girl or boy in the class to their kid's birthday party, and the kids all generally like each other and are willing to play with anyone who wants to.

Anyway, at this particular sleepover, we camped in tents in the backyard, and the invitation had said to bring your sleeping bag and pillow. Bernadette forgot her pillow on the floor of my mom's car and didn't realize it until we were getting ready for bed, so Claire offered to share her pillow. Bernadette declared, loudly enough for all the other girls in the tent to hear, that Claire's pillow smelled bad. Claire appeared hurt and embarrassed by this. I took Bernadette to the birthday girl's mom and asked if she had an extra pillow, and she gladly gave her one.

In eighth grade, Bernadette was asked out by a boy Claire liked, and she got super mad about it, even though Bernadette rejected him. She thought Bern had been trying to spite her or something by flirting with him, so she told Bern that she and Colleen were going to fight her. They said to meet them at the bottom of the hill that this ice cream stand sits atop near our neighborhood at 4:30 in the afternoon on a Friday. The bottom of the hill leads into the Rocky River Valley.

Bernadette asked me to come with her. "I've never fought anyone though, unless you count tackling Colleen O'Rourke during touch football at recess," I said to Bernadette with a laugh. Colleen was a really cocky kid. She thought she was the best at everything, especially sports. One day, while covering her, feeling all amped up and tired of her attitude, I decided to tackle her. Seeing how shaken she was from it, I kept doing it, until she asked me to take it easy with a quivering lip.

Bernadette said, "I've never fought anyone either. That's why I need you. You at least know some boxing skills. You'll probably be a natural."

So I agreed to go. We skipped and sang Misfits songs on the way to the valley, neither of us letting on to be even a little afraid. I remember it feeling more like we were on our way to take care of some bothersome, mundane chore that we could get through with good music and a can-do attitude, like deep-cleaning the bathroom, than on our way to possibly get our faces punched in.

Claire and Colleen never showed. We waited nearly two hours for them, just sitting in the grass, talking. We decided that was long enough and left to get ice cream.

My drink was almost gone. I scanned the room. There was a peppering of people I'd known since way back when—some from school, others old neighbors. I didn't have an inclination to approach any of them but wouldn't detest making polite chit chat if they approached me. There were lots of people my dad's age who I didn't know but probably knew him or his family, and there were the flat-cap-wearing Irish guys.

I ordered an amaretto sour next. Had a second one. Ordered a Long Island. Got sick of all the sweetness, so went back to vodka with Sprite. Even the Sprite was too sweet though, so then I switched to Rolling Rock, which I used to chase the rum shots I also bought.

I left the bar inebriated with a spontaneous urge to walk. I walked away from the pubs, past the coffee shop, the big antique clock at the corner of the street, and the gas station and shopping center across from the clock. Then I was into the blocks of houses.

I came up on Holy Rosary. It looked smaller and powerless in its emptiness at night. In those harder junior high years, it loomed before me menacingly as I waited outside of it in the morning for the first bell to ring, upon which we'd be let in. My stomach would start cramping once Bern and I were close enough to hear the shouts from the gaggles of kids and the whistle of the crossing guard on our morning trudge there. I'd climb the stairs to the junior high with dread, uttering a myriad of desperate words to myself in my mind. *Maybe I'm only dreaming I'm in school right now and I'll wake up in my bed, on Saturday. It'll be over before you know it. Take it hour by hour. Once you get to lunch, the day will fly by.* I only felt safe when Bernadette was attached to me or when we were in a lesson since no one was permitted to talk and I could turn all my attention to the material.

I approached my parents' street. I wondered what the chances were that the back door was open. I could see myself pushing through it and being greeted by their sleepy-eyed dog, her tail wagging. She never felt like my dog because they got her as a puppy only a year before I moved out, a little after the dog my brothers and I grew up with passed away, but she knew me. She'd follow me to my old room, which had been made into a guest room, and lie beside me in my childhood bed to let me stroke her back and scratch behind her ears before trotting off to my parents' room to fall back to sleep. Then, I'd drift off into an unstirring, dreamless slumber.

No, but I can't go there, because I'll have to explain to my parents in the morning, and it'll probably startle them to find someone in the spare bed, as I'm sure they'll wake up before me. I brushed the idea away and continued on.

I soon reached St. Ambrose. It was tradition for women on my father's side of the family to go there. I was part of the third generation to attend. My mother and her sister had gone there too, and Grandma Vivian had served on its board of trustees.

The gothic building that is the academy sits atop a cliff overlooking the Rocky River Valley. The school was established by an order of nuns in the late nineteenth century and is still overseen by the order's current sisters. They live in a convent, called the mother house, across from the school and connected to it by an underground tunnel that runs into the first floor. There's a wooded trail beyond the front lawn, which leads to a cemetery where nuns are buried.

I found the academy to be enchanting with its archaism and surroundings of lush forestry. It made me feel as if I were at Hogwarts. Each day that I walked the halls and outside grounds, I tried to picture how they might have looked in the years my relatives had walked them. I could almost sense their presences, imagining their teenage selves lingered perpetually in a parallel universe.

To stay out of the light from the streetlamps lining the academy's driveway, should any police be patrolling the area, I crept through the lawn to the side of it. Sneaking onto the grounds reminded me of sneaking *off* them with Bernadette. It was an independent study day in our jazz class, meaning we could take the whole 80-minute block period to work on whatever we wanted. On those days, Bern and I normally hung behind the stage in the auditorium and jammed out to our own music. Our teacher, Mr. Henry, didn't mind at all when we wandered out of his sight.

This particular time, Bernadette said she was sick of everything and wanted to go someplace else, and maybe we should try to, so we did, and we succeeded. To enter through the school's side door, you had to buzz in, but you didn't have to buzz out to leave from it. Guess St. Ambrose never figured any of their students would be delinquent enough to attempt skipping. We ran, giggling, all the way to the sidewalk along the main road. Then, we boarded the 75 and went to the mall. Jazz was our last class that day anyway, so no teacher but Mr. Henry would have noticed our disappearance, and he never mentioned it. He was probably too busy worrying about one of his adulterous affairs with a student, as he was later found out to be having. Come to think of it, they were likely why he scheduled those independent study days. Sure, he was giving private lessons all right in that windowless office of his with the door locked. Eww.

I stood in the concrete circle outside the front steps of the school and mother house where parents dropped off and picked up their daughters. Emptiness and darkness served the architectural style of the buildings well.

At Holy Rosary, I'd tell myself that things would be much better once I got to high school. The opportunity to go St. Ambrose had felt like a precious gift. I remember how I'd sit at the desk in my room at night with the materials I received the day I shadowed there as an eighth grader—the shiny, white folder with the school logo on it carrying the mustard-colored papers showing course listings, clubs, and sports teams, the clicky logo pens. I'd glide my hand over the lettering of the school name on the front of the folder and carefully take out the mustard papers, trying not to crinkle them or stain them with oils from my fingers. I read them over about a hundred times. I kept a sheet of notebook paper in the folder too, on which I'd written lists of courses I'd like to take, in order of most like to least, for each year, and a list of clubs I was interested in joining, ranked in the same fashion. My selections of those classes and extracurriculars seemed so life-shaping at the time. Funny enough, by the end of high school, it was all trivial to me, dwarfed by college, and then the hallowed idea of the college experience became similarly dwarfed by the real world.

I moved on into the grassy area behind the patio where we'd eat lunch when the weather was nice. I went all the way to the cliff at the edge of the campus that leads into the valley. I'd climbed down it many times before with the cross-country team to go for trail runs. Bern and I joined for a couple years for fun.

With the light of my phone to guide my way, I descended the side, slipping occasionally on the decaying leaves, sticks, roots, and muddy soil that the side comprised of and puncturing my hand on a particularly sharp stick.

Once in the valley, I crossed the road to get to a trail I knew. As I began walking the trail, I looked for sycamores and at the moonlight glittering on the river that ran along it. I could walk this for miles, for cities, like all those drives Desmond and I took, I told myself. I could walk until the sun is up.

When I found a group of sycamores, situated in a nearly perfect circle, I slid my hand down the uneven, papery trunk of one. Then, I slid my whole self down until I was resting against it on the ground. My head was still ahum with intoxication and getting sleepy, my thoughts twisting into nonsense as they do between consciousness and dream state in my bed at night. I finally gave in to letting my eyelids fall. Thankfully, I'd worn my winter coat and accessories and didn't get too cold overnight.

I was awakened later in the morning by an intense urge to vomit. After I did, I crawled away to a cleaner area, where I sat with my back to a boulder and became aware that it was raining and the fact that I'd basically fallen apart, as I told you about earlier.

Desmond had texted and called a bunch of times, wanting to know where I went and if I was OK. I told him I'd met up with Gabby at the bar and crashed in her dorm and that I'd be back soon.

Once I was stable enough to stand without getting sick, I walked as inconspicuously as I could to the trail, waiting until I didn't hear any approaching footsteps before appearing on it. I went up the same side to get out of the valley that I'd gone down.

When I reached the top of the cliff, I turned to admire the view, since I could now actually see it in the daylight. Nature has always had a way of giving me perspective. The strong, sure voice of my conscience cut through. I hadn't been able to hear it so well in a while. It told me, you could be standing on the edge of greatness, or you could be standing on the edge of the fall to your demise. To build the life you used to dream of, you need to break out of the relationship you've been caught in for so long. It's like you're on some spinny carnival ride that never shuts off. Jumping from it seems frightening and dangerous, yes, but riding cycle after cycle is making you sick. You have to devise a plan for how to leave and carry it out soon, no matter how hard and scary it feels, even if Desmond keeps threatening to tell your parents things you want to hide from them or take you to court, and even if it breaks your heart, because none of those things could be as bad as the way you might end up if you don't do this.

TWENTY-FIVE

My dad called one day while I was in class. I let the call go to voicemail. I had another class right after, so I checked my voicemail as I was walking there.

"Hey, Dani," he paused. "Grandpa Adrian had a stroke. A bad one." I stopped in my tracks, right in the part of the innerlink running through the bustling Student Center.

He went on, sounding softer and choked up, "You need to come to the hospital as soon as you can."

Tears streamed down my face. I didn't care that anyone saw me this way, including one of my professors who happened to walk by. I called my dad back to get the hospital information and left immediately.

I found my mom, Uncle Marty, Aunt Jackie, Grandma Margie, and Grandma Vivian in the waiting area outside Grandpa Adrian's room. I kissed and hugged them all. Grandma Vivian's brown eyes were twinkly and red from crying. She sobbed heavily with her chin dug into my shoulder and a wrinkled tissue pressed over her mouth and nose when I hugged her.

The heavy sobbing would start back up each time another family member arrived.

My dad, Mikey, Jenna, and her husband of about a year were sitting in some chairs along the wall of Grandpa Adrian's room when I tiptoed in. They all greeted me with hugs and kisses too. Then I went to my grandpa's bedside. He didn't look himself. His cheeks were sunken in, his hair uncombed and slightly matted in the front. His skin looked thin, his hands boney and feeble. To see him like this was shocking. I'd never seen anyone lying in a hospital bed on the fringe of their mortal life before. I'd been fortunate enough not to have lost a close relative yet.

"You can hold his hand if you want. It's all right," said Jenna. "He can feel your touch and hear you talk to him. He hasn't been able to fully open his eyes, but he tries to sometimes. The meds have him really out of it."

I timidly placed my hand over his, which was resting at his side with his fingers curled into his palm. I felt more at ease once I made contact, and I gave his hand a squeeze.

"Hi, Grandpa. It's Dani." I felt stupid, being unsure of what else to say. I thought what I said should be something profound, and I was getting timid again with everyone listening to me, but I tried over. "I love you so much, Grandpa. I feel like I've never thanked you enough for all you've done for me, so, thank you, for everything. You know, you've been one of the biggest positive influences in my life."

Suddenly, his hand opened, and he gasped. Startled, I pulled away. With slow, trembling fingers, he felt around at his side, like he was searching for something.

I reached back out to him, and this time, he squeezed my hand. He began gasping again, and two tears rolled out of the corner of his eye.

Now Jenna and my dad were crying too, which gave me a lump so big in my throat that I couldn't speak anymore. I stood by Grandpa Adrian's bedside until his breathing calmed, his hand loosened and fell away from mine, and he seemed to drift back into a sleep state.

Jenna and her husband left the room to get some coffee, so I then took Jenna's seat next to Mikey, who'd been sitting silently with his hands folded in his lap. When my throat was clear enough for me to talk without sounding like a hiccupping frog, I said to my dad, "So where and when did this happen?"

"This morning, at home," my dad said. "He was supposed to go into the store today, but he never showed up. An employee called his cell, and there was no answer, so they called Vivian's cell. She left for work before him. She told them the last she knew, he was getting ready to go to Carmin's, so she rushed back home, and she found him on the bathroom floor."

"God. Poor Grandma."

"The doctor said it shouldn't be long until he goes," my dad said in a hushed voice. "Maybe a week. They've cut off food and fluids."

In case my grandpa could hear, I also turned down the volume of my voice, all the way to a whisper. "Wait, so they're *making him* die by depleting him?"

"Well, with the severity of the stroke, he wouldn't be able to recover well enough to fully sustain himself, so, his quality of life wouldn't be good, and he probably wouldn't have much time left anyway. This is pretty standard practice in cases like this, honey," said my dad.

"Is he in a lot of pain?" I asked.

"I'm not exactly sure how much he can feel. They've been pumping him with meds to minimize pain as much as possible. By the end, I don't think he'll be able to feel anything anymore."

"I guess that's good," I said.

I visited Grandpa Adrian two more times in the hospital. As he diminished, his breaths became shallower with greater gaps between them, and they came more from his stomach than his chest. A nurse told us that's the sign someone's very close to passing. He took his final breath on a Friday. Grandma Vivian and their children were the only ones in the room.

Mom and Aunt Jackie gave the eulogy at the funeral Mass. It was the most beautiful story I'd ever heard—one of adventures and the great love Grandpa Adrian had for my grandma and the family that they built together.

My brothers sat in a line to my left, my dad after them at the end of the pew. Bernadette came home for the funeral, and she sat to my right. I cried harder than I ever had in my adult life, harder than I knew I physically could. My whole body tensed up and shook, and I kept having this involuntary heaving when I tried to take a deep breath that hurt my chest.

At the cemetery, after we'd all placed our flowers on the casket, my parents stepped arm in arm beneath a tree in the distance. My mom buried her face in the breast of my dad's suit coat and cried in long, pained wails that echoed through the cemetery. He wrapped his arms around her and kissed her head. I sighed heavily with heartbreak for my mom as I walked back to my car with Jenna's arm linked in mine and Bernadette beside me. I wished I could become the tree, scoop her up with my branches, and rock her to sleep.

A family friend who owned at Italian restaurant held a reception after the burial, free of charge. After the reception, our family went to my grandmother's house. Uncle Marty broke out Grandpa Adrian's whiskey and started passing around shots. Everyone took one but Jenna.

"You're pregnant," Grandma Vivian stated with certainty.

"Well, we weren't going to say anything yet, but yes."

"Your news is the sun breaking through on this gloomy day," said Uncle Marty. He planted a kiss on Jenna's cheek and shook her husband's hand.

We made a toast to Grandpa Adrian's life and the new one that would be, because of him, a part of him. When Jenna gave birth to a daughter the next year, they named her Adrienne.

Standing there after our toast, happy to see everyone else looking happy for the first time in a while, I decided that among whoever you call family, whether they're blood or not, also isn't a bad place to be when it's your time to go. I wondered if I'd ever find someone I could build a family with that would feel like the one I'd known. For better or worse, it really was something special.

When I went home, the rest of my plan was clear. I asked Mikey to meet me at my house with his pickup truck early the next morning. He went to a trade program several times a week with later hours, so he was home most mornings. He said he could come at eight, and I told him that was fine; Desmond would be long gone to work by then.

We loaded my large essentials—a dresser, a night-stand, and music equipment—into the bed of the truck. There was no time for careful packing. I wanted to get out of the house quickly and with little fuss. And besides, packing would have given me away to Desmond. I duct taped the drawers in my dresser and nightstand shut. I piled all the clothes from my closet in the trunk of my car and tossed my shoes in a heap in front of them. I put my bathroom products, knick-knacks, and other small items that belonged solely to me and that I couldn't part with inside a couple duffle bags I had. I decided everything else—the furniture Desmond and I bought together, the wall art, dishes, silverware, cleaning appliances, linens—would all have to stay. There wasn't anything we shared that I felt I needed to trouble myself with stuffing in a vehicle at the cost of moving slower, and I wouldn't take what hadn't been mine to begin with. Well, except for Lee. Considering it was mostly me who took care of him and loved him, I thought it was fair that we stay together.

Before walking out of that house for good, I left Desmond a note on the dining room table saying that if he really wanted to fight me for Lee, he'd have to come over to my parents' place to do it. I folded the note in half so I could enclose my share of the rent for the next two months, since my name was still on the lease. I'd started asking other servers at the restaurant for their shifts once I made the decision that I was leaving and also sold some old music gear to come up with the full amount. I told Desmond I was working more to save for a new guitar and maybe a vacation for us so he wouldn't get suspicious and upset. Our lease was up in a couple months, so my hands would be washed of it after those last payments, and Desmond could either renew or not without me.

I sat Lee in the passenger seat of my car. I turned the key in the ignition and then patted his head. He stared at me in a light pant that made the corners of his mouth curl softly like a grin, the sun illuminating the marble-y, gold-brown irises of his relaxed eyes.

"Lee. Short for Lovely," I said to him, and we drove away without looking back.

Mikey had already put down the tailgate of his truck and was sliding my dresser across the bed when I pulled into my parents' driveway. I got out of my car and helped him lower the dresser to the ground. Then I asked, "Did you tell Mom or Dad that you were bringing my stuff over today?"

"I mentioned it to Mom," he answered.

After we carried the dresser inside, I took Lee into the backyard to get acquainted with my parents' dog. Mikey got the rest of my stuff out of his truck and put it in my old bedroom. I brought the things from my car in later. It all just barely fit with the furniture my mom had added. There wasn't space to do much else but open the dresser drawers and walk a narrow path from the bed to the door, but that's all I really needed.

My mom got home before my dad. I was sitting in the living room watching the dogs play when she walked in.

"I've got a couple of strays here I see," she said.

"Hi, Mom," I said. "This is Lee. I know I've mentioned him to you before. He was Desmond's, but he sort of became mine. Is it OK if we stay here for a while? He's a really good dog, and you won't have to do anything for him. I'll take care of him on my own."

"Yes, you both may stay here," my mom said. "It never stopped being your home you know, and it never will. No matter what."

TWENTY-SIX

At the beginning of my last semester of college, we were assigned to pitch topics for a long-form narrative journalism piece. The finished product was to be between 20 and 30 pages and would count as our final.

The professor teaching the course was someone I had before. He stopped by the table where I was packing up my notebook and papers at the end of class the day he gave the pitch assignment and said, "Miss Moran, I had an idea for your long-form piece. I enjoyed the one you wrote previously about the department store. I'd like it if you built upon that topic. I think there's a lot there. You could go into the history of the store, downtown shopping before suburbanization, and the drama within the company. You could write it like a historical drama show. And use your great-aunt as a primary source."

"My grandma."

"Right—your grandma."

Grandma Vivian and I arranged to meet at her house for an interview one Friday evening. I told her

I'd bring dinner. She said she had a craving for wonton soup, so I got Chinese. She answered the door with her usual "Hellooo!" The table was already set with porcelain plates, silverware, napkins, and glasses of water when I came inside.

Since my grandfather passed away, Grandma Vivian had been keeping herself exceptionally busy with work, and when she wasn't working, she stayed occupied doing favors for family and friends, always finding some project.

With only Grandma there, the house and everything in it strangely felt smaller. It was like I'd come back to look at a place I hadn't seen since I was a child and the dimensions were all different than in my memory.

We had our soup, then dumped our chicken and rice from the cardboard cartons onto our plates and ate that too. Afterward, Grandma Vivian made coffee. Once we poured it and fixed it how we liked, I turned on my handheld recorder.

"So, what was your first position with the company?" I asked.

"I started as a sales associate in the Junior Misses Department at the flagship store downtown when I was in high school," my Grandma replied. She explained to me how she climbed all the way up to Executive Vice President by the age of 34, then later, Chief Operating Officer.

"No one like me could ever do what I did nowadays," she said. "I never went to college. I just worked my ass off, learned on the job, kept proving myself, and any time a higher position opened up, I went for it. I believed I needed the positions more than everyone else because I had small children at the time. They helped inspire my work ethic. Today, corporations don't let you do anything without a degree. It's important, but it's not."

Next, I asked, "What did you like most about working for the store?"

She said, "Because of the type of place it was, working there, you learned to appreciate beautiful things and what something fine is. You looked for quality. I really liked that. It was just an elegant time when I was employed there. Women always dressed up. Men too—they went out in suits. Downtown was really alive, and our store—all the shops downtown, actually—did elaborate window displays. You went downtown to see it. The buildings were gorgeous. In ours, the elevators were brass. The chandeliers were crystal. The floors were marble. It was both dazzling and intimidating to me starting out there, having grown up poor. It's amazing to see the way the city's reinvented itself and come back."

"So what led to the stores' closures?" I said.

She went on about how the company was eventually acquired by some slimy liquidator. He promised their employees and vendors that he wasn't closing the stores, then tried to bribe my grandmother with $1 million to start letting employees go and continue ordering high-end merchandise that he could put in a warehouse for his other retail chain headquartered in Cincinnati. He told her in private the reason he'd bought the company was because they owned all their properties and he wanted their real estate.

"Of course, I refused the bribe," Grandma Vivian said. "I took out a $15,000 ad in *Women's Wear Daily,* exposing him and apologizing to all our employees and vendors, and I told our vendors to stop shipping merchandise to us. The Cleveland media went nuts over it. There were news crews at the house every day for weeks. Your mom, she was so funny—she'd shut the door on the camera men. Your grandpa would hide out in Carmin's." She broke into laughter. "He'd call every hour when he was working evenings asking me, 'Can I come home yet? Are they all gone?' He was patient through it all. The drama. The stress. The long hours I had to put in to keep things going strong when I was running the place. He was there for all my joys and successes with it too. We celebrated those. And our company parties—uh," she put a hand over her heart, "we had great parties. Your grandpa and I held the Christmas party every year right here in the house. You couldn't even move, there'd be so many people."

My grandmother's eyes glossed over with a wistfulness. "I'd always say to your grandpa, 'We wear so many hats.' We were often hosts for our family and friends—you know, we had the gathering house. We were parents, we became grandparents. We each ran a business. And of course, as a couple, we had our own intimate world together."

"Yes, you both always had full plates. I'm impressed with how much energy you guys had leftover to chase us grandkids around your house."

"Well, you find the energy and time for what's important. Your grandfather lived for the weekends with his grandkids."

I smiled.

"So, a little off topic—I understand you're not living with Desmond anymore. You're back at home with your mom and dad?"

"Yes, that's right."

"Were you two not getting along?"

"No. Not really. I mean, I guess we never really did. I wanted it to work so badly because I loved him, so I kept holding on. And sometimes it did seem good, but that always wore off quickly. Desmond can flip so easily."

"Well, there'll be someone else for you. You're young. Consider your relationship with Desmond a learning experience. You know, no matter what hat your grandpa was wearing, he was the same person—good natured and loving. He never changed when we were behind closed doors. He always treated me well."

"That's really good to know."

I was silent for a moment, meditating on her words.

"By the way, Grandma—I've been meaning to ask you … Could you show me again how to make your sauce and meatballs?"

"Of course. Same time next Friday work for you?"

"It's a date."

TWENTY-SEVEN

At the end of the school year, I began applying for writing jobs, writing for anyone about anything. I wanted to start working my "real job" immediately after graduation. One day, I got a call from the HR Manager of a marketing agency downtown that I'd applied to called Gerstenmaier Marketing. They had a large and impressive portfolio of clients.

Just hearing, "Hi, Dani. This is Bob from Gerstenmaier Marketing," got my heart pounding with elation.

He went on, "I'm calling to schedule an interview with you for the copywriter position you applied for. We received 287 submissions for this job, and you are one of only four people out of the lot that the Editorial Team wants to meet with, so you should be very proud." And I was. At the time, it was the most validating thing anyone had ever said to me.

For hours after our conversation, I was incapable of focusing on tasks, my head a hot air balloon that had floated away from the rest of my body. I spilled some laundry onto the bed for folding but found myself scrubbing dishes before the folding was done, not remembering why I'd wandered into the kitchen in the first place, and I abandoned the dishes without thinking to begin organizing my purse. I finally gave up on trying to be productive. Instead, I sat on the front porch swing with cold green tea and submitted to my daydreams of a career and an exciting new beginning.

Bob told me he'd meet me in the atrium of Gerstenmaier's building on the day of my interview to escort me to where I needed to go. Wedged between an Italian bakery and a hotel, the building was 13 stories with a stone front and three gold-trimmed entranceways with revolving doors. The atrium had a bistro, a Starbucks, and lots of sleek, black-and-white arm chairs and end tables in the center. The floor was made of old-fashioned tiles—shiny, beige, and hexagonal. A grand staircase with a gold railing curled up to the lofty second level, which was a gold-railing-lined hallway with office windows and elevators overlooking the atrium. The ceiling was Victorian-style with intricately-engraved crown molding and bronze tiles.

A man came toward me. It was Bob. He said, "You look lost, so I'm going to guess you're the girl I've been waiting for, Ms. Moran."

I said, "You guessed right."

As we walked to the elevator, he told me about the tenants on the second floor—a radio station and a city development group. Gerstenmaier was on the seventh floor. I'd always been partial to the number seven, so I took it as a good omen. Then, Bob talked of all the agency's benefits: getting to work from home when you're sick, have an appointment, and every Friday, free coffee, being just a short walk from great restaurants and coffee shops in case the free lounge room coffee didn't suffice for my taste buds, 10 paid holidays a year, 20 paid vacation days. Medical. Dental. 401k.

When we got to seven, Bob pointed out the two lounge areas where employees could go to get away from their desks and find inspiration or work collaboratively. Through the glass door of one of them, I could see couches, big windows, lots of natural light, shelves of books, and a TV on the wall.

Bob brought me to the office of the Editorial Director, where she and the Writing Manager were waiting for me.

The director's name was Sandra and the Writing Manager's name was Dave. They were both very smiley as Bob handed me off to them. They invited me to sit with them at a small, round table there in Sandra's office. She had a stack of papers in front of her. I saw that my resume was on top.

"We were impressed with your writing test, Dani," she said, pulling it from beneath my resume. Along with submitting a resume, application, and cover letter, job seekers were asked to write advertisements for 10 given topics as a test of skill. Sandra skimmed over the first page of ads I wrote, then flipped to the second page and did the same as if she was refreshing herself on the content. I could see the document was marked up and that comments had been written in pen. I couldn't believe that some people—people with name plates hanging outside of downtown offices—had so carefully considered my work. *My* work. Printed it out and stapled it together for the world to see, touch, and judge.

"Yes, we see great potential here, which is key in our selection process," Sandra said. Dave nodded along in agreement.

They started asking me the interview questions next—why would I like to work there? What is my writing process? What do I enjoy writing about most? Where do I see myself in five years? I was surprised by how confident and charming I sounded in my answers and how instinctively they came to me.

At the end of the week, Bob called me again to tell me they wanted to offer me the position and would be emailing me an official offer letter. I accepted. My start date was scheduled for two weeks after graduation.

Bernadette came home for a month before starting a job in Denver. On the evening of the day she got in, we walked to the valley with thermoses of wine for an intense catch-up session.

"Do you remember when we went to the valley to fight Claire Zajac and Colleen O' Rourke and they never showed? And then we got ice cream?" said Bernadette.

"Of course I do," I replied. We sat in the same spot we did the day the fight was supposed to go down.

I told Bernadette about some of the things that had led to my breakup with Desmond and about the pregnancy. She asked why I didn't call her for help with any of it, appearing stunned and hurt. I said I didn't know; I guess I felt I should handle it myself.

Gabby moved in with Cameron after graduation. She didn't start looking for a job in her field right away.

Instead, she kept bartending. She told me she didn't think she was ready for the cubicle life yet, or maybe ever, and wanted to search her options more first. Search herself. We decided we wouldn't continue Ardis Alchemy. Maybe we'd start up a new project together, depending where our creativity and moods took us.

I went to visit her where she and Cameron were living. It was an old house, and pretty big, with a former storefront attached to it. One of the roommates—they had, like, eight of them—inherited the house from a grandparent. The inheritor, a self-proclaimed anarchist, fancied the place a commune. He was big into dumpster diving, always bringing home food from dumpsters behind restaurants and grocery stores. He'd make a spread of his findings on the sales counter of the storefront for his roommates and crashing friends to have at.

When I got to the house, bodies were strewn about all parts of the mismatched furniture in the living room—a worn, brown leather sofa and a couple of cloth recliner chairs. Other people were on the floor. All the lights were off. Some indie rock artist I didn't know was being blasted through a speaker in a corner of the room. The walls were white and held posters of numerous artists, among them, Bob Dylan, The Beatles, Lou Reed, and Ernest Hemingway. There were various brown and black scuff marks on the white paint, and the edges around the ceiling had yellowed from cigarette smoke. The carpet looked decades old—a color like goldenrod with some areas of it darker than others. The faded light of the setting sun sneaking in between the halfway-pulled-down blinds and the thick window panes gave the tinged room a greenish glow.

I was standing uncomfortably in the living room full of unappealing strangers, having no clue where Gabby had disappeared to, holding a Rolling Rock, when I felt a touch on my shoulder and was compelled to turn around. My heart skipped a beat. There before me was Liam McDaniel.

"Liam, what are you doing here?" I said.

"I live here," he said with a laugh.

"You do? Gabby never mentioned that to me."

"Well, to be fair, I just moved in this afternoon. I only brought one box. I'm going to bring the rest of my stuff tomorrow. So ... how are *YOU*?"

"I'm really good." I backed myself into an empty space on the floor and sat down cross-legged. Liam followed. "I just got hired as a copywriter for Gerstenmaier Marketing downtown."

"That's really awesome. Congratulations! Good that you'll be using your degree," he said.

I thanked him and asked, "So ... what are *YOU* doing now?"

"Eh, working at Best Buy still, trying to figure out my next move. I felt I needed to get out of my parents' house for a while, so we'll see how it goes here."

"Did you take the MCAT?" I asked.

"No. I'm now debating whether I should start studying for it though," he replied.

"Wait—when did taking the MCAT become debatable? I thought med school was the plan."

"I thought so too," Liam said, disappointment in his voice, "but the closer I got to graduation, the more I became unsure of it. Do I really want to be a doctor, or do I just like the title? That's what I've been wrestling with. I'll have to pay for grad school on my own, so that would be a hefty chunk of change for something my heart isn't in."

"Do you have any other ideas for what you might like to do?"

"Maybe become a teacher. Or go back to school for environmental science. Or see if there's something I can do in the field of environmental science without going back to school."

"OK. Well, at least you have some direction," I said, trying to sound supportive and understanding.

"Everyone! Hey, everyone! May I have your attention, please?" Cameron yelled over the music. One of his cronies turned the speaker down low. Cameron thanked him.

He pulled a chair from the dining room into the living room and stood upon it.

"Since we have a nicely-sized gathering of people here, I'd like to call the first official meeting of Pissed Off Grads—POGs for short—a movement I'm starting. I'd love if you could lend an ear and hope you'll be interested in joining me, but if not, carry on merrily with whatever you're doing," Cameron said.

"Is he for real?" I asked Liam.

"I believe so," he answered.

"What has driven me to start this movement is the unacceptable reality for college graduates," Cameron continued. "We've gotten degrees, so tell me, where are the jobs? We shelled out an absurd amount of money for educations that the establishment said would set us up for success. Now we have mountains of debt with no careers to show for them and help us pay our debts off. Universities don't really care how we do out in the world after we graduate. Their promises to prepare us for the workforce are empty. They're only after our money. They've lied to us and robbed us all. We must end the corruption in higher education for future generations and demand that our debts be forgiven."

"Wasn't Cameron an Acting major? Did he not realize how tough of a field he'd be going into?" I said to Liam as Cameron began laying out his strategies for rallying more people in the community around his cause for rebuilding the system.

"Yes, he was, and I don't know," said Liam.

"No one forced him to choose Acting. If he didn't want to deal with the adversities of the creative life or was looking for his education to provide a direct path to a job, he should have picked a more practical degree or gone to trade school. What has he even done to try to get an acting job? Has he gone on any auditions?" I said.

"I don't recall him mentioning any, so no, not to my knowledge." Liam answered.

"Well, a diploma can't go on auditions for you. Or fill out applications, or do interviews. Effort still has to be put into landing a job after the degree is earned."

"This is true," said Liam.

I supposed Cameron thought himself so special and different that casting directors would show up at his door.

I threw my head back to empty out the last gulp's worth of beer from my bottle.

"I'll be right back. I'm going to get another drink," I said. I'd put my six-pack in their refrigerator.

Gabby was standing in front of the sink with her back turned to me when I approached the kitchen. At the sound of my footsteps on the sticky tile floor, she spun around.

"You scared me," she said, her mouth filled with food, her hand to her heart. "I was starving. Want some nuggets?" She picked up a plate of chicken nuggets from the counter and held it out to me. Her eyes were bloodshot and hazy with a sad, distant twinkle in them. Stars burning out, they were.

"No, thanks," I said. They looked like they could be McDonald's dumpster nuggets.

As I reached for another Rolling Rock, Gabby said, "Hey, I'm sorry I didn't warn you about Liam. I didn't know he'd be here until today. I should have told you when I found out."

"Oh, it's OK. Really," I said. "We're actually catching up. It's going fine."

"Yeah, it looked it when I saw you two together. I just wanted to double-check that you're all good."

Gabby suddenly looked up toward the ceiling, unblinking, like she was listening for something. Cameron's rant about his struggle was drowning out anything else that could have been heard.

"His struggle ..." Gabby scoffed. In a lowered voice, she said to me, "His dad, who he'll barely speak to, paid for his college, and he puts $1,000 in his bank account each month." She rolled her eyes. "Anyway, we need to catch up later too! I want to hear more about this new job!"

"OK." I smiled. "Later, for sure."

I only saw Gabby a few more times ever again after that night. She became increasingly flaky about hanging out and eventually stopped responding to my calls and texts.

As I was passing through the dining room, I noticed the door to the storefront was open. Curious, I wandered inside. Loaves of bread and pastries were laid out. One loaf had blue mold.

When I got back to Liam, he said, "Hey, do you want to go somewhere quieter? I know a place."

I told him, "Sure. Lead the way."

He took me to a bedroom upstairs. It was in the point of the house, so the ceiling was very low and slanted, and the windows were at floor level. There were two beds in it.

"One of these beds will be mine. There's another guy who stays in here. I actually can't tell which one he sleeps in. They say he almost never comes home, so the whole sharing a room thing shouldn't be too hard. This is what I wanted to show you." He pushed a window open, stepped through it, and held his hand out to me. I took his hand and joined him on what was a small deck overlooking the backyard. He shut the window behind us.

"Much quieter," I said, feeling satisfied with this new location. "So, are you planning to join Cameron's crusade?"

"I don't know about that, but I do think he secretly enjoys being unemployed so he has more time for it—for *POGs*," he said, further emphasizing the name with spirit fingers, which made me snicker.

"POGs ..." I echoed. "Oh my god."

"*That's* his job now. He needs something to be loud about. Love the guy, but yeah, he's something."

I suddenly remembered a conversation I had with Desmond in high school. A boy from his class had run away. The whole community was in a panic. The police found him a month later in the woods near his house. He'd gone off train hopping for a while, and when a route brought him back home, he decided to live in the shelter of a thicket. When word got around both our schools about his return, Desmond had said to me about it, "Fucking rich kids. They all think it's cool to be poor. Bunch of wannabe beatniks."

Liam sat down, his back against the window. I sat beside him.

"Ah, Dani Moran," he said, looking at me, "now a bona fide career woman."

I smiled sheepishly at the floor boards, feeling I was being teased.

"I *am* happy for you, but I'm honestly having a hard time picturing you in a corporate environment. I don't know that it suits you. It's not very rock 'n' roll. Won't your soul get hungry?"

"I don't know," I said. "What I do know is that if I don't have money for food, my stomach will get hungry."

"Touché."

"From how it was described to me, I don't think the job will be half bad. And I'm sure it won't be forever. I'm looking at it as a stepping stone. What I need most right now is independence, and I think this position will help me get it. I don't want to rely on anyone for anything—not my parents, not friends, not a boyfriend."

"I understand," Liam replied. "You shouldn't feel like you can never ask your parents for help though. You didn't choose to be born. They brought you into this world. That means they don't get to just write you off when you're 18, in my opinion. If I had kids, I wouldn't do that to them. You know, in other parts of the world, it's totally normal for an adult to live with their parents until they're married off."

"I'm sure my parents would let me stay with them longer. I want to prove to myself that I can go it alone is all," I said.

"OK. I can respect that. As long as you know you're not really alone."

We were silent for a moment. Liam looked deeply into my eyes. I shifted my gaze to my shoe laces.

"So you're not with Desmond anymore, I take it?"

"No. I left him."

"Good. I would rather have seen you with someone who treated you right, even if it couldn't be me, than see you with him."

"Love makes you do things that don't make sense." I shrugged. "I guess I got myself pretty mixed up."

"The same boiling water that softens the potato hardens the egg. In other words, your circumstances can break you or they can make your stronger. Muster up that toughness that I know you have inside yourself to become the stronger person. Channel the negativity you've been feeling into something positive."

I laughed. "Who's that quote by?"

"I believe Mel Robbins."

"I've missed your words of wisdom. And yes, what you said is what I'm trying."

"Do or do not. There is no try. Yoda."

I rolled my eyes, pretending to be unamused. I caught Liam staring deeply into them again. I thought he might be about to lean in for a kiss, so I looked straight out at the night sky.

Later, he did work up to leaning in for a kiss. I let him place it perfectly on my lips, and then I kissed him back.

We ended up sleeping together in the bed that he thought would be his. We locked the door, figuring the guy who was never around wasn't going to come home, and we were right.

Liam and I saw each other regularly for two months before I cut things off. I wasn't sure if I truly loved him or had only started things back up with him because he made me feel secure and cared about, as I'd longed to feel. I knew he wasn't one for casual encounters, and I didn't want to lead him on.

A couple weeks after beginning as a copywriter, I decided I needed to buy decorations to put on my desk. I found some antique and locally-handmade trinkets at a favorite store of mine that Jenna had introduced me to on the west side of Cleveland. As the cashier was ringing me out, I told her how the specific items I was purchasing were to make my workspace at my new job with Gerstenmaier Marketing homier and that I couldn't believe I actually got it and that their building is just so beautiful. I was still too over the moon about the opportunity to help myself. She looked at me with alarm, like I might be about to start talking to the cup of pens next to the register about the weather and retell her what a fairy whispered in my ear, so I shut up.

On my way home, the main street was unusually busy. Crowds of people were trying to cross to get to the church, and I realized, why, of course—the festival is this weekend. I had a knee-jerk reaction to pull down a side street for parking. I followed behind the mobs to the large banner hung between two telephone poles in front of the church driveway with "St. Francis Festival" printed on it in red and green. The telephone poles were also stuck with red and green streamers and balloons. The parish was in the old Italian neighborhood where Carmin's had been. No one else in the family was able to run the store after my grandfather passed, so my grandma sold it.

I walked down a long line of food stands. The air was heavy with the smell and heat of frying dough. It was the first time in my life that Carmin's didn't have a stand there. In the years Bernadette and I worked in the store, we came up to the festival in the afternoons to take food orders.

I bought stromboli and gelato and ate them on the curb of the churchyard in front of Saint Francis of Assisi's statue. Afterward, I wandered through a row of games. There were the same ones as always—the fishbowl toss where you win a goldfish, the baseball throw, the prize wheel, the high striker game with the mallet, the game where you throw darts at balloons, the dunk tank, the utility pole for the greasy pole climb. And then there was horseshoes in the strip of lawn behind the church, the bocce court, and past both of those, in the continuation of the parking lot that serves as a recess area for the school kids on weekdays, were the few rides. I got in line for the Ferris wheel.

Sitting at the top while they were filling more carts, I put too much thought into how high up I was, and I got a rush of anxiety. It had been a long time since heights freaked me out. It had been a long time since I'd ridden a Ferris wheel.

Once, I rode that Ferris wheel with Grandpa Adrian. I was going into first grade. Grandma Vivian brought me up to the festival that day. Grandpa Adrian took a break from his stand for a while to do some activities with me, leaving one of his employees in charge, while Grandma Vivian played a game of bocce with some old friends. She was quite a competitive player.

Anyway, Grandpa Adrian and I were suspended in the air, waiting for the ride to start, and he was explaining to me how the greasy pole climb works. "They cover the pole in axel grease, and then each team tries to make it to the top. They can climb on each other to get there, like a ladder. Now, the winners, they go on to the Olympics, where they face winning greasy pole teams from all over the world. They train all year round for this."

A strong breeze came and tipped our cart forward, and I didn't care for it. I turned my head away from my grandpa and used the crook of my arm to cover my eyes.

"Don't be scared, sweetheart," he said to me. "We won't fall. This thing's sturdy. Just wait 'til we get going. We'll have a great time. You'll see."

But I was still unsure.

"Dani, someone's trying to wave to you. Look over here, honey. It's OK," Grandpa Adrian said.

I cautiously poked my head up.

"All right, good. Now, see right there?" He pointed down below to Grandma Vivian.

I could faintly hear her calling to us, "Hi! Love you!" She took her camera out of her purse and snapped photos of us waving back and blowing kisses.

As I was thinking on which album or box my mom might have those photos in, I sensed a presence next to me. I entertained the idea that it was Grandpa Adrian's spirit; he'd come to join me again. I looked over at the empty space on the seat and smiled.

The carts were filled up and the ride began to really move. Feeling calmer, I challenged myself to look down. I laughed at how painless it actually was. Then, I fixed my gaze on the tops of the trees, their thousands of leaves swaying and glittering in the sunlight, and the infinite clear sky, all part of something more liberating, comforting, inspiring, thrilling, fascinating, enchanting, capable of bringing about reclusiveness or coalescence, and utterly complex than any virtual reality that could ever be constructed, yet, so simple. How sweet it is to just watch the world on a summer day … What a rarity of inner peace and joy.

In that moment, it was also so simple to accept the inevitable imperfections and mysteries of life. There was a warm swelling of big-heartedness in my chest. It swallowed up the combativeness I was carrying in the name of my convictions, and I wanted no more polarization between me and anybody.

I don't need to shut out or spit fire at everyone whose perspectives differ from mine, nor do I need to fixate on changing their minds, I realized. Owning our bodies and what is within them, as I believe we do, means we also own our thoughts, so by that principle, we all have the right to think however we wish to. Respecting freedom of conscience and honoring each other's human dignity seem like they should be easy, and they should be enough.

If we let it, hatred can circle forever and destroy everything around us, so I won't hold grudges or seek vengeance, and when a twinge of malice is felt by my imperfect nature, I will not act on it. My goodness can overcome. And perhaps if I stop holding on to animosity for all who don't empathize with me and fearing the sting of their words, I'll experience inner peace and joy more often.

Now, when I feel like everybody is against me and I want to throw rocks and my fists, I remind myself of these sentiments.

TWENTY-EIGHT

My first apartment was in an old Tudor building near a shopping and dining district called Coventry Village in Cleveland Heights. I had a one-bedroom suite on the fourth story, which was the top story. An elevator was never installed, so Lee and I had to traipse up and down many steep, narrow stairs. I promised Lee I'd carry him once they became too difficult, since he was growing old. I cursed every day that I realized I forgot something in my apartment once I'd reached the ground floor and had to go back for it.

The stairs were just one of the idiosyncrasies of that apartment. The kitchen was barely wide enough to bend over and open the oven door. I often bumped into the refrigerator doing so. There was only a single window air unit, in the living room, so the living room would feel like a walk-in freezer while the rest of the place was balmy, and the unit would loudly spit small ice chunks at night, which sounded like glass shattering on the hardwood floor. The first time I heard it, I thought someone was smashing my windows or dishes. I came running out of my bedroom wielding a pocket knife.

But, oh, how I loved that place. I'd sit on the window seat in the living room, and in a journal, I'd write lyrics for my solo project songs and what I thought could perhaps be the workings of a novel, and I'd dreamily stare out over the courtyard and the neighborhood beyond it. Lee would be in his bed next to the window seat, surrounded by his new toys. Scented candles would be crackling away on my book shelf and music from my speaker echoing off the high ceiling. Every so often, I'd pause my writing to gaze at the vintage-style poster art on my walls, and I'd feel so sunny and inspired.

I never expected playing music by myself to feel that different than playing with a band. At my first gig in a coffee shop near my place, I almost chickened out. I was just about to start, and I looked at all the full tables and got stage fright—something I hadn't experienced in many years. I realized that backing down in front of all the people staring at me would be almost as humiliating as having a shaky performance, so I forced myself to stay up there. Nobody walked out in the middle of my set groaning or laughing, and afterward, people clapped, so I thought, let's keep working on this solo thing. If you can do this on your own, there's nothing that you can't. I found comfort and strength in seeing that I am all I need to make things happen; I'm enough as I am.

I soon settled into a workday routine. I'd park in the garage by the hotel, and before going into the office, I'd stop at the bakery next door. I always bought a cappuccino. Sometimes an egg sandwich too, or when

I felt like treating myself, a pastry. The guy who ran the counter, Vince, learned my name and my orders. The guy who worked in the back—I imagined he was Vince's father or uncle—would give me a nod if he saw me when I came in. I liked being a regular somewhere.

Working at Gerstenmaier remained a novelty to me for a while, but I did start to see how someone could grow tired of corporate life. Someone like me, anyway.

The hustle could be really thrilling. I especially enjoyed the rush of the city sounds on the morning commute, during which I'd pass through the thriving medical district and the redeveloping Midtown neighborhood, hastening through the grand atrium with the delightful inflated sense of importance it gave me, and being seen around town in my office clothes that made me feel smart and sophisticated.

But the hustle was also draining. I'd be sitting in one of the lounge rooms, brainstorming copy in solitude, and I'd think, there's almost no reason to be here—no reason to spend any time or effort trying to get smart-and-sophisticated-looking in the morning or battling traffic or searching for parking to do autonomous work that can be accomplished just as efficiently in the comfort of my home. And there were days when I did yearn for something else to feed my creative spirit. I'd find my mind wandering from my sales copy to more ideas for a potential book and pulling new song lyrics out of nowhere that would demand to be written down.

I said, perhaps someday, I *will* only work at home, for myself. I'll be my own boss—a novelist. Or a book editor. Or I'll start a copywriting business. Or I'll be a music journalist, spending more time at shows than I do a desk, or a political journalist, spending my time instead on the House floor. Maybe later, I could run for public office myself. Maybe I could even be anything.

Our histories are behind us. We shouldn't forget the bad parts lest they be repeated, but we must forgive and move on from them so they don't crush our future potential, and so the fights already won will not have been in vain. I can't control everything, but there's a lot that I can, for I am capable, and because today, I have the same rights and freedoms as everyone else around me. Since understanding all this, I stopped feeling defined by my past adversities and pain, but rather, by my triumphs and what makes me happy.

As I was waiting for my cappuccino one morning, a young, handsome, dark-haired man in a button down, trousers, and tie said to me, "I see you here a lot. Cappuccino, right?"

I was slightly embarrassed for some reason that he'd caught onto my habit of ordering a cappuccino.

"I've also noticed we see each other here a lot. And yes, I got a cappuccino," I said.

"Must be good. I'll have to try it sometime," he replied.

"You should. Everything I've ordered here has been good. It's a good place! I guess another reason I always come here is for the nostalgia it gives me. My grandpa had an Italian grocery store with a bakery in it, and I worked there growing up."

"Oh," he said, smiling at me with twinkly eyes. "My parents have a grocery store too. They sell Mexican food. They were both born in Mexico. I worked there growing up as well. I'm a financial analyst now."

"Oh, wow," I said. "What's their store called?"

"Delgado's."

"I'll have to go there one day."

"Get the pork tamales."

"Will do."

"What's your name?"

"Dani."

"I'm Alex. So, Dani, I know some other good places to get food. Maybe I can take you to one sometime for dinner."

I blushed and got really warm. Is he asking me out? Yeah right. He seems like a catch, so why would he be interested in me?

"Oh, uh, yeah. Maybe sometime. That would be nice," I said.

I noticed my drink was waiting for me. I hadn't even heard Vince say it was up. It was like everyone and everything in the room besides me and Alex had dropped back and blacked out. It was just the two of us talking in the hot spotlight of a stage.

I grabbed the drink and said to Alex, "Have a great day," then quickly walked out the door. I immediately felt like an idiot. Did he think I'd politely, and awkwardly, rejected him? I hadn't meant for it to come off that way. I wanted to say yes.

He was looking at me through the window as I turned in the direction of the office. I waited for him to step out of the bakery so that I could ask for his number.

I was still rebuilding my confidence when it came to dating. I was still rebuilding in many other ways, but I'd come far.

I would never be the same as I was before. I'd be so much better—a victor who could be held down by no one other than myself.

AUTHOR'S NOTE

I acknowledge that domestic abuse occurs in all types of romantic partnerships, to include same-sex partnerships, and that women are also perpetrators. The intention of this story is absolutely not to portray men as the sole perpetrators of domestic abuse or to stigmatize men or masculinity in any way. I find men to be pretty fantastic. Researchers believe that men largely do not report domestic abuse or even discuss it due to social reasons, which I won't get into here but encourage you to look up if it's a topic that interests you. I wrote this story in the perspective of Dani Moran simply because I liked how her voice came out on the page and how natural it felt to be in her head; she was an instinct.

While I've written about the Catholic Church with some criticism, I do not discount the vast amount of charity that the Church and its followers bestow upon the world or the Church's inarguably virtuous teachings, such as compassion, forgiveness, and loving your neighbor. The Church is not my enemy. In this book, the complexity of the Catholic identity in the modern world is representative of the complexity of all humans, which Dani tries to make sense of along her journey.